The Lincoln Inn

by Dr. Michael R. McGough

Foreword by Gregory M. McGough

D1114652

Thomas Publications
Gettysburg, PA 17325

This book is dedicated to:

Brady Charles Pitzer
Gabriel Michael McGough
Olivia Francis Pitzer
and
Tina, my real-life Tinasia.

Contents

Foreword

Although the Lincoln Inn exists only in the imagination of the author, the inspiration for the Inn and the location on the Tuscarora Mountain described by the author are both very real. In the words of the author's son, the inspiration is clearly explained.

To The Reader,

I have fond childhood memories of our many trips to Johnstown, Pennsylvania, to visit my grandparents. We lived in Biglerville, which is also in Pennsylvania, and the trip to Johnstown took about three hours. Although there are several possible routes, Route 30 is among the more direct. Along the stretch of the Lincoln Highway that we traveled, were steep and winding climbs up several mountains, one of which was the Tuscarora Mountain.

On one of these trips I had an asthma episode as we were heading up the Tuscarora. I had medication, but cool air also provides relief. My dad found a spot to pull off. In an instant, he was standing beside me outside the car. The air was crisp and cold, and snow flurries filled the night sky. Not knowing what else to do, he rubbed my back and reassured me that I would be fine, and in short order I was.

Childhood asthma can be a scary thing. Although he did not tell me at the time, I'm sure my dad was a bit scared that night too. At the top of the Tuscarora Mountain on that winter evening there was not another soul besides my mother, my sister, my dad, and me. My dad said he wished there was a restaurant or an inn nearby where we could have stopped and relaxed for a bit, but there was none.

My father has always had a unique ability to see through negative circumstances. His way of dealing with tough situations and his recollections of them later have always demonstrated the positive perspective known only to the optimists among us. My dad wished there had been an inn near the top of the Tuscarora Mountain for us that night, so in the cheerful reality of the optimist that he is, he imagined one to be there. The story he told me that night to calm me down was about his imaginary inn. That story was as warm as an apple-log fire in his Lincoln Inn and I appreciated it.

Since that night in 1984, my dad has helped many young people relax and learn in his imaginary Inn. Stories from the Lincoln Inn are sincere and kind. A visit to the Lincoln Inn is a unique experience and all visitors are welcome. Even though the Lincoln Inn only exists in my dad's imagination, stories from the Inn can offer comfort and a pleasant rest to anyone on the journey of life!

The light is still on and the Inn is open and ready to welcome anyone wishing to visit!

Gregory M. McGough

Introduction

Last week I sat in front of the biggest birthday cake I've ever seen. It had to be big to hold a hundred candles. This big cake had my name on it. "Happy Birthday Mac" was written right through the middle of the maze of candles. Mac is what everybody calls me, but my full name is Abraham Francis McGettegen. Just like I'd done so many times before, I made a wish, and I blew out the candles. It took me three tries, but I finally did it.

There were a lot of people in my house, and they were all welcome. Family, neighbors, folks I see all the time, and even some old friends I'd not seen in years took time to come and help celebrate my 100th birthday. We celebrated most of the day and into the evening. It was a special day for me, and I was sorry to see it end.

When the last of the guests left, Tinasia and I just sat for a spell. Tinasia is my wife. She's only 97. Compared to me, she's just a kid. We've been married for 77 years, but we've known each other as long as either of us can remember. You see, her daddy, Mr. Graffenburg, owned land on the east side of the Tuscarora Mountain. He cut timber off the land and ran a small saw mill. My daddy, Francis McGettegen, bought a piece of land from him in 1893 and built a country inn that opened in April 1894. He and my mother called it The Lincoln Inn and that's been the name of our place ever since.

The Inn has been home to me all my life, and Tinasia and I have no plans to leave. The day after my birthday we retired, and we retired The Lincoln Inn too. After a hundred years, we thought we could both use a little rest. For the past week, we've done a lot of reminiscing. The Lincoln Inn, or Lincoln's Place as some people call it, has a very interesting history. Tinasia and I can recall all but the first few years. We've had a good life here on the mountain, and we've provided a really nice place for folks to eat and spend a night or two.

Unfortunately, we can't recall each and every one of our guests from the past century. But there are a number we remember as vividly and clearly as though they were here just yesterday. They gave us memories worth keeping, and we've enjoyed recalling them from time to time. During the past week I decided that a memory worth keeping is a memory worth sharing, and that's just what I'm gonna do. Tinasia has agreed to help me.

The Lincoln Inn

The Lincoln Inn sits along the Lincoln Highway, on the east side of Tuscarora Mountain. McConnellsburg is five miles to the west, and if you travel east on the Lincoln Highway, you'll be in Chambersburg in 17 miles. All of these places are in the middle of Pennsylvania toward the south where Pennsylvania meets Maryland at the Mason-Dixon Line.

For a long time the road in front of the Inn was called the Chambersburg & Bedford Turnpike. The "pike," as the locals once called it, connected Chambersburg in the east with Bedford to the west. The turnpike was built by a private company in the early 1800s, and travelers paid a toll to use it. The toll was just a few pennies, but the people who built the road still made good money. The road was nothing like a road is today. Back then it was nothing more than just some dirt tracks in many spots, and measured about 56 miles from one end to the other. It took two days to go that far with a good horse and in good weather. Back when it was built folks thought it was a modern road.

Around 1913 somebody got the grand idea that there should be a road that went from coast to coast. They wanted a road that would connect the Atlantic Ocean and the Pacific Ocean. Because automobiles were becoming popular with folks, there had to be roads for them to drive on. It took several years to complete this coast-to-coast road. In some places the road had to be built, but in other places they just used stretches of roads that were already there. The old Chambersburg & Bedford Turnpike was a stretch of road that they used. My daddy was really pleased about that because his Lincoln Inn would sit right along the new road.

Road builders made a hard surface on the road in front of our place during the summer of 1915. The new paved road was named the "Lincoln Highway." It was kind of a memorial to President Lincoln, for all he did during the Civil War. Later on, when there were so many roads in the country that they had to be numbered, our road was called U. S. Route 30. Daddy said we were lucky to live on a paved road. He said people could come to the Inn no matter what the weather was like.

Our Inn was named for Mr. Lincoln long before the highway was named. My dad really admired Mr. Lincoln. He was always proud of the name he and my mother gave their country inn. And he was never bashful about telling folks that he named the Inn long before the Lincoln Highway was named. A few times, I even heard him tell folks they got the idea for the name of the highway from our Inn. By the way, my first name is another example of Daddy's fondness for President Lincoln. I never asked my parents, but I often wondered if they might have called me Mary, if I had been a girl. That was Mrs. Lincoln's first name.

When travelers would ask my dad the quickest way to get to some place along the Lincoln Highway he'd say, "Well, you could take Route 30, or you might want to consider the Lincoln Highway." And if it was some place between Chambersburg and Bedford, he'd say, "And then again you might want to think about taking the Chambersburg & Bedford Turnpike."

Thoroughly confused, they'd ask which route was the best. Daddy would smile and say, "Huh, it really doesn't matter because they're all the same road any how!" If my mother heard him, she'd just smile and shake her head. Regardless of the name, it's still a road today. Most people just call it "Thirty," but some people still remember it as the "Lincoln Highway."

The Lincoln Inn, Lincoln's Place, or just the Inn as we call it, was built with timbers and lumber right from the mountainside where it sits. The big stones used for the foundation and the fireplace in the lobby also came from the mountain. Daddy often told guests, "Every stick and stone in the place came right from this mountain!" Mr. Graffenburg milled the lumber for my dad and helped him design and build the Inn. That was the beginning of their lifelong friendship. They were both hard-working men and they respected each other. I don't know as I can remember even one harsh or angry word ever spoken between them.

I have no idea where the original color scheme for the Inn came from, but for some reason it was sacred to my parents. My mother, Arlene McGettegen, confided in me once that she considered a change, but couldn't even bring herself to suggest it to my father. So for the past century, Lincoln's Place has been a rustic brown color, with dark green shutters on the windows, and a porch railing of the same green color. They were always colors that seemed to match well, and they blended nicely with the forest setting we enjoyed.

The Inn was built from a simple design idea, figured out by Daddy and Mr. Graffenburg. It had two floors with a small attic above and a cellar below. The first floor had ceilings that were ten feet high, so the rooms always looked a little bigger than they were. On the first floor there was a big room. In this big room was our dining room and a big sitting area. In the front corner to the right of the main doors as you walked in stood the registration desk.

Behind the dining room there was a big kitchen where the meals for guests were prepared. Behind the kitchen were our rooms. We had a small parlor and three bedrooms. Our parlor, or living room, had a large window that looked out into the forest behind the Inn. It was fun to watch the seasons change through that window. There was a bedroom for my parents, a bedroom for me, and a bedroom for my sister Grace. We had a bathroom too, and that was rare in 1894. Most people still had a privy; you know—an outhouse.

Upstairs there were eleven guest rooms and six bathrooms. Five bathrooms were each shared by two rooms. The biggest of the guest rooms, the one that was at the end of the great hallway, had its own bath. My mother always said that was the Presidential Room, and that's a whole story in itself.

Inside the Inn, most things were red, white, or blue. My folks both had a really strong streak of patriotism. The Fourth of July was always a big day for us. Daddy once told me if he had it to do over again, he'd have waited to open the Inn on the Fourth of July. As it was, he and my mother opened Lincoln's Place in early April of 1894, the same month I was born.

In the lobby, on the wall behind the registration desk, there has always been a picture of President Lincoln. It was a copy of the last picture ever taken of him. I think Daddy told me once that it was taken just four days before Mr. Lincoln was shot at Ford's Theater, on April 14, 1865.

The negative for the picture was one of those old types made on a glass plate. Someone must have dropped the plate, because there was a crack that ran along the top of the picture. It really didn't hurt the picture much, because you could still clearly see Mr. Lincoln's face. The picture is in a simple black wood frame. There are two mats around the picture. One is red and one is blue, just like alot of things in the Inn.

The Inn has always been a comfortable place. People have enjoyed staying here and eating the rather simple meals we've served over the years. Mom was a great cook and Tinasia is every bit as good in the kitchen. We've enjoyed our century here, and we hope to keep enjoying the place a good bit longer. As I said before, the Inn and I are just about the same age. That's why we're both retired now.

The First Guest

The Lincoln Inn has had many guests over the past century, but I guess a good place to start would be with the very first one. I was not an eyewitness to this visit, so I'll try to tell it as it has been shared with me over the years.

The spring of 1894 had been particularly cold, and there were no travelers calling at The Lincoln Inn. Mr. Graffenburg and my dad started the Inn during the summer of 1893, and finished in March of 1894. Mr. & Mrs. Graffenburg had been down to eat a few times, and my uncle from Johnstown had stopped to see my folks for a few hours on his way to Baltimore.

No guests meant no money, and for a while Daddy said he worried about how he'd pay the bills. For a time, he often recalled, he thought it may have been a mistake to build an inn in the middle of nowhere. The little bit of money he and Mom had put back had to be used. Even though he was nervous about what he'd do for money, he kept busy around the Inn. Once in a while he helped Mr. Graffenburg at the mill.

The Inn was one of the first places in the area to have electric lights. Even so, it was usually dark at night during that first spring in 1894. Daddy was trying to save money on electricity. He and Mom had some kerosene lamps they used. I know one of those old lamps broke years ago, but I think the other one is still around here somewhere. From time to time we'd need them when the power went out during an electrical storm.

On April 15, a storm the likes of which had never been seen around here before, came west over the Tuscarora. I've heard accounts of snowfalls that measured anywhere between two and four feet. Daddy said he knew for sure there would be no guests at the Inn for quite a while. But as he soon learned, there was one guest he was forgetting about.

Late in the evening of April 17, I decided it was time to make my grand entry. They didn't expect me to be born until the beginning of May, but I had other plans. I've always enjoyed setting my own schedule. I guess this is a habit I picked up early on in life.

The road was still impassable because of the heavy snow, and Daddy decided it would not be safe to try and take my mother down the mountain to the doctor. The Inn was one of the first places on the mountain to have a telephone, so Daddy got a call through to Dr. Buckman in McConnellsburg. He was only five miles away, but the trip up the mountain could take several hours. The snow was so deep, Daddy was afraid Dr. Buckman would not be able to make it at all. When my dad called him, Dr. Buckman told my dad he had a horse that was more cooperative than most, and he would leave right away. He asked Daddy to leave a light on, so he could find the Inn.

There was a sign on the front of the Inn that read, THE LIN-COLN INN, and there was a silhouette of the bust of President Abraham Lincoln on it too. There was a small electric light over the sign. Daddy said he turned that light on for Dr. Buckman. Fortunately there was a full moon that night, and warmer air blew up the valley from the south. Dr. Buckman, or "Buc" as Daddy called him, arrived about dawn. I was born early in the morning, and by noon Buc was on his way back down the mountain.

My timely arrival made me the first guest at the Lincoln Inn. Daddy said that later in the day the Graffenburgs came to see me. They didn't know it then, but 23 years later I would become their son-in-law, when I married their daughter Tinasia. She was born three years later in 1897, on the 25th of July.

Buckman's visit to Lincoln's Place that day was the first of many for him. You see, my sister Grace, born just two years after me, married Buc's son, who also became a doctor. He and my sister still live in Bedford, about 40 miles west of here.

The Inn was rather quiet the day I was born. Dad said Mama and I slept most of the day. He said that before he went to bed that night, he walked around the Inn just checking the place. When he reached up to turn off the light over the sign out front, he decided to leave it on. He said the Lincoln Inn was now open for business, because the first guest had indeed arrived. He and Mother wanted their Inn to be a welcome spot, a place where people would want to stop, so the light was left on. It was on all the time, day and night, to welcome travelers no matter what time they passed.

Except for times when the power went out, or when the bulb burned out from time to time, that light above our sign was never off. Daddy even put a small cover over the switch so we wouldn't turn it off by accident. When the Inn was rewired in 1951, that switch didn't have to be replaced. It had never been used, so they just left it there, covered like it had been for more than half a century.

Last week, before I went to bed on the night of my 100th birthday, I took the cover off that switch, turned it off, and put the cover back on. My dad put the cover on the switch so nobody would accidentally turn the light off. Now I'm gonna keep it there so nobody accidentally turns it back on.

Tinasia, the Inn, and I are all retired. We all need a little rest and we've certainly earned one. For the last few years, we had help running the place, but even with help it got to be too much. We tried to sell it, but we really didn't want to, so our hearts just weren't in it. You see, this isn't just a business to us; this is our home too. And besides, nobody seems to be interested in making the commitment Daddy, our wives, and I made to this place. So after a century, the Lincoln Inn is closed, for good.

50th Reunion

The man who pulled up in front of the Lincoln Inn could not help but notice me staring at his car. I had good reason to stare, because it was a beauty. "I'm Everett Summerhill of Austin, Texas. Do you have any rooms?" he asked as he got out of the nicest car I had ever seen. I guess I did not answer quickly enough, nor did I take my eyes off the car. Closing the door and walking toward me he said, "She's a Cadillac Torpedo, finest car on the road."

"I can surely see why," I answered, still staring at the car.

"I say, do you have a room for the night?" Mr. Summerhill asked again in a louder and more distinct voice.

"Yes, yes sir, I'm sure we do. Can I help you with your bag?"

The rather short and thin Mr. Summerhill started making his way toward the Inn. As he did, I noticed an obvious limp. He really favored his right leg. "Let me take your bag sir," I offered.

"No need, this limp is older than you, and I can make it just fine. Got it at Gettysburg fifty years ago. A Yank hit me when I wasn't looking," he said with half a grin.

Mr. Summerhill went into the Inn and was greeted by my father who was watching the desk. "Can I help you?" Daddy asked.

"Yes you can, if you have a clean room and a good meal," Summerhill answered, flashing a big Texas smile.

Extending a hand to shake the outstretched hand of the Texan, Dad replied, "We only have clean rooms, and as long as my wife's doing the cooking, we'll be serving nothing but good meals."

Mr. Summerhill set his single bag down in front of the desk and signed the guests' registration book. "What brings you our way, Mr. Summerhill?" my dad asked. He was curious about folks, and was never shy when it came to asking our guests about themselves. Before he could answer I blurted out, "He's a Civil War veteran from Texas, and he got wounded at Gettysburg fifty years ago."

Starting the next day there was going to be a big reunion in Gettysburg. It was scheduled to last four days, starting on July 1. The year was 1913 and it marked the 50th anniversary of the battle. This was the second big reunion since the battle. There had been a 25th anniversary reunion in 1888, and now this one. There was also one in 1938 to mark the seventy-fifth anniversary, but like I said, this story is about the fiftieth in 1913.

"The boy is right. I'm here to go to the reunion tomorrow," Mr. Everett Summerhill said. As he spoke, he leaned on the counter and something in the pocket of his loose-fitting white shirt clanked against the desk."

" I've only ever been out of Texas twice—once to serve the Confederacy during the War and now to come to this big reunion they're having in Gettysburg. To me there's no place like Texas, and there aren't many good reasons to leave."

"That's kind of how I feel about Pennsylvania," Dad added.

"Which way to my room young man?" Summerhill asked.

"We'll put Mr. Summerhill in room five Mac," Dad told me.

"Follow me, sir. It's just up the stairs," I said, picking up the bag in front of the desk and walking toward the steps.

"You're determined to carry that bag, aren't you," Mr. Summerhill said with a chuckle. "I guess you're looking for a tip. Well, here's one for you," he said, flipping me a silver dollar.

After helping Mr. Summerhill settle into his room, I went back out front to get another look at his Cadillac Torpedo. I checked it over really good. It was the most handsome car I had ever seen, and I had no reason to doubt that it was "the best car on the road," just as Mr. Summerhill had suggested.

As I was about to go back inside, another car pulled into our front parking lot. A tall man got out. Like Mr. Summerhill, he too looked old enough to have fought in the Battle of Gettysburg. I asked if I could carry his suitcase and he just nodded, indicating that I could.

The monogram on the well-worn suitcase read, "Dr. Robert D. MacNamarra, The Pennsylvania State University." If I had been a bit more observant, I would have known that Dr. MacNamarra was a Union veteran. I can still picture the regulation blue G.A.R. flannel suit he was wearing, but at the time I did not know why he was wearing it.

The G.A.R. was the Union veterans' organization known as the Grand Army of the Republic. They had adopted sort of a uniform suit for their members to wear. They could buy them in a lot of different stores or order them through the Montgomery Ward mail order catalogue.

As we approached the desk, I introduced Dr. MacNamarra to my father as if I had known him for years. I assumed he was Dr. MacNamarra, but I guess he could have been someone else. Maybe he was a friend who had borrowed the suitcase from Dr. MacNamarra, in which case I would have looked rather silly. "It's always good to have a doctor in the house," my dad said, turning the registration book toward the guest.

"Thank you, but I'm not a physician. I was a professor of history at Pennsylvania State University until I retired," MacNamarra said in a quiet voice. "If one of your guests becomes ill," he continued, "I could read to them or lecture on a number of subjects, but there is little I could do to tend to their ills."

Even though he had no reason to be, I think Daddy was a bit embarrassed. So he quickly changed the subject. "I see you're a Union veteran as well," he said, for he recognized the blue G.A.R. suit Dr. MacNamarra was wearing.

"Yes I am," MacNamarra said, picking up the pen with his left hand and laying his right arm heavily across the guest book. "My family thought I should have a new suit for the reunion at Gettysburg."

"And a fine suit it is Professor," my dad added, "right down to those brass G.A.R. buttons." The professor just nodded a silent "thank you."

"Mac, take our distinguished guest to room number eight. I think he'll be comfortable there."

Dr. MacNamarra and I walked up the steps rather slowly. When we reached the door of room eight, I opened it and took the suitcase inside. "If I can get you anything Professor, just let me know."

"No, I just want to rest a bit, but thank you just the same," the Union veteran said, holding out his left hand to shake my hand. He caught me a bit off my guard, because I was accustomed to shaking hands with my right hand. We shook our left hands, and in so doing he passed me a tip of fifty cents. I know that does not seem like a lot today, but in 1913, that was a nice tip.

As I went back down the stairs, I said to myself, "I hope all the fight is out of those two, or things could get really interesting at dinner."

Some other Civil War veterans had stayed with us over the past two weeks, but they had already made their way to Gettysburg. The actual reunion did not start until the next day, but there were all kinds of special events both before and after the formal celebration. Something as big as the Fiftieth Anniversary of the Battle of Gettysburg had to be celebrated over more than just four days, and it was. As I remember, some of the veterans stayed around for weeks after the actual reunion was over.

Around the Inn we always tried to eat around 5:30 in the evening. Mama figured that was a good compromise for folks who usually ate at 5:00 and folks who ate at 6:00. Daddy used to say he never thought it mattered much. He said if folks were hungry, they'd eat no matter what time it was.

On that June evening in 1913, Mr. Summerhill was one of the first guests at the table. Some other folks had checked in during the day, and as I recall, all of the rooms but two were full. The friendly, smiling Texan who had arrived just a few hours ago had become an unhappy looking man with a scowl on his face, when he came to the table. He did not try to strike up a conversation, and the look on his face was a warning to others to "leave me alone."

Dr. MacNamarra came down to dinner in more comfortable clothes that were definitely cooler. He had taken off his regulation blue Grand Army of the Republic suit. The professor took a seat at the big table near Mr. Summerhill, nodding to the former Confederate soldier as he sat down. He had no idea that Mr. Summerhill was a Confederate veteran. He was just trying to be friendly.

Summerhill's scowl quickly turned even more ugly. He abruptly stood up and walked to the other side of the table, where he took a seat. Even though he had not said a word, he clearly let Dr. MacNamarra know that he did not wish to sit near him.

The retired history professor made no gestures in reply, but instead picked up the folded white napkin on the table in front of him, unfolded it, and laid it across his lap. We had no idea what was going on, but everyone at the table sensed that something was not right between these two men. There had been some small talk going on, but Summerhill put a quick end to all that.

At this point in my story, I guess I should tell you what we think happened. Even though the Inn is well built, there is no insulation in the walls. It is just a well-made wooden structure, and guests in their rooms could hear almost everything that was said in the big room downstairs. In summer it was even easier to hear, because most guests kept their doors cracked open a little so the cool breeze from the mountains could circulate through the rooms. Because of this, we have always believed that Summerhill heard Professor MacNamarra come in and register. He also heard that he had been a Union soldier at Gettysburg. Okay, back to the story.

Mom came out of the kitchen and announced, "I hope you folks are hungry for fried chicken and meat loaf!"

In a somewhat nervous voice, Daddy said, "Sure smells good, Arlene." Everyone else was quiet. The tension was mounting by the minute. Mr. Summerhill had made an odd and embarrassing move, and everyone seemed to be waiting for him to make the next move, too. In short order he did. He broke the awkward silence when he abruptly said, "I'll have mine out on the veranda." I later learned that "veranda" is a word, commonly used in the South, that means a porch. "There's no way I'm gonna eat with a Yank. Never have and never will!"

The question in all of our minds as to what the problem was with Mr. Summerhill had been answered. Plainly, he refused to eat with a Yank. In case you do not already know, "Yank" was a nickname the Southern soldiers had for the "Yankees" of the Northern army. The Yanks in turn called the Southern soldiers "Rebs" which was short for "Rebels." There was nothing really mean about the nicknames, but they were not exactly friendly either.

Dr. MacNamarra never looked up. Mother had set the meat loaf in front of him. Quietly he helped himself to a piece and passed the plate to his right. No one else at the table knew who the angry Texan was referring to. Not wishing to cause an even bigger scene, my mom quickly fixed a plate for Mr. Summerhill and took it out to him on the side porch. He offered little more than an abrupt and rude "Thanks."

A lady sitting near me was quite concerned about what Summerhill had said, and asked. "Did someone say something to offend that gentleman?" Since the folks were all sitting at his table, my dad felt responsible for giving an answer. He said, "I don't think so. I do know that he was a Confederate soldier at Gettysburg." Daddy knew he was referring to Dr. MacNamarra, but he did not want to say.

"I think the gentleman was referring to me," the gentle-looking, retired professor of history said. "You see, I too fought at Gettysburg, and I fought on the Union side. He must have heard us talking when I registered." The professor said nothing else and went back to his meal. He seemed neither offended nor concerned.

Daddy tried to make small talk, but everyone around the table was feeling a bit uncomfortable. You know how you feel when something like that happens. Even though you are not directly involved, you still feel bad for the people who are. Twice my mother went out to see if Mr. Summerhill needed anything, and twice she was greeted with a short, "Nope, I'm fine."

In short order, the guests finished their meals and headed back to their rooms or the front porch. No one went out on the side porch, knowing they would encounter Mr. Summerhill. Everything was quiet, and then out of nowhere, Mr. Summerhill thought it time to speak his mind. He came in from the side porch, and walked right up to Dr. MacNamarra. He and Daddy were the only two people remaining at the table. They had been talking about the Pennsylvania State University, where Dr. MacNamarra had taught history for almost forty years.

"I stayed out here, pretty far from Gettysburg, so I wouldn't have to spend the night with any Yanks. The only reason I'm even going to this reunion is to honor the Confederate cause and the men who died for it. I've had a bum leg for the past fifty years because of a Yank, and I got no time for you or your kind."

MacNamarra never moved or said a word. He just looked at Summerhill. Then Summerhill said, "You Yanks never knew what we went through." Reaching into the pocket of his shirt, Summerhill took out a minie ball. That was the name of the lead bullets fired by Civil War rifles. "That's the one that got me. A Union slug that left me crippled for life. I've carried it with me every day for the past fifty years, and I don't ever want to forget what Mr. Lincoln's army did to me."

I had been sitting on the steps, and when Summerhill mentioned Lincoln, I could not help but look at the picture of President Lincoln that hung behind the registration desk. I remember thinking to myself that it was strange that he picked the "Lincoln" Inn of all places to stay. And then he explained why.

"I picked this place because I thought it was far enough away from Gettysburg," Summerhill snapped. He grew more and more agitated as he talked. Dr. MacNamarra's silence seemed to be angering Summerhill more than anything the Union veteran could have said.

"I'm not here to forget or forgive," Summerhill said. I sensed that Daddy was getting concerned about where this was all going.

He stood up and Mr. Summerhill got the message that he had gone just about far enough. MacNamarra had yet to say a word.

"I'm sure you have some unpleasant memories, Mr. Summerhill, but this is hardly the time or place to bring them up. And Dr. MacNamarra doesn't deserve what you're trying to pin on him. He was, just like you, fighting for a cause he believed in." I have always admired Daddy for taking up for Professor MacNamarra.

"All I wanted was a stupid peach pie." That was how Mr. Summerhill replied. His comment made no apparent sense, and Daddy gave him a rather puzzled look in return. Then Summerhill continued. "We hadn't eaten since we marched out of Chambersburg. And when we did eat, the food wasn't fit for the horses let alone soldiers. When things got quiet on our end of the line on July 2, I walked up to a farmhouse and found a peach pie high on a shelf in the pantry. I figured when the folks who lived there left, they didn't see it cause it was up so high."

Mr. Summerhill interrupted his story to tell us that General Lee had warned all of his soldiers that they could take what they needed when they were in Pennsylvania, but they were not to harm the civilians, damage their personal property, or steal things they had no real use for. Then he continued.

"Just as I reached for that peach pie, the only food in the house, I felt burning in my leg."

Summerhill had lowered his voice and pulled out a chair. A little of the anger had left his voice. Some of the other guests had come back in from the front porch, and Summerhill continued. "They say you never hear the bullet that hits you, and that's as true as it can be. The next thing I knew I was being carried to a makeshift field hospital. Dying and dead men were all around me. It made me sick in the stomach. They put me on a table that was nothing but a door on top of two sawhorses, and a doctor dug this bullet out of my leg." Summerhill took the minie ball from his shirt pocket and laid it on the table. It was at that point that I figured out what had clanked on the counter when he was registering.

Folks had taken seats around the table again, and I had moved up a little higher on the staircase so I had a good seat. Dr. MacNamarra was leaning back in his chair with his left arm behind his head, and his right arm lifelessly hanging at his side. Mom had brought out some cups and was pouring coffee.

"I was sick for days. I got the fever and it was really bad. Back then there was nothing they could do for us. You either sweated it out or died." Summerhill moved a little closer to the table, and pushed the lead slug around in a small circle as he continued. Even from where I was sitting, I could see that the minnie ball had a big gash in the side of it. I wondered what caused that, and almost as if he could hear my thoughts, Summerhill said, "That's where it hit my bone." He took the nail of his thumb and rubbed it along the gash in the lead.

"That was the end of the War Between the States for me," Summerhill said. Daddy later explained that the Confederates never called the war the Civil War. To them it was always the War Between the States. "After I was able to move, I made my way back to Texas. My family had money, so I was cared for, but I never did get the full use of my leg back. Leaning back in his chair and looking at the ceiling, Mr. Summerhill said out loud just what he was thinking. All I wanted was a lousy pie and what I got was a bullet from a Yank."

"What you said about not hearing the bullet that hits you is correct," Professor MacNamarra said in a gentle voice. "You weren't the only soldier shot at Gettysburg. My right arm has been of little use to me over the past half century."

There was an awful silence in that room. The North and the South, the Yanks and the Rebs, the Union and the Confederacy had met again. The personal tragedies of their war were once again clearly visible, even fifty years later.

For everyone else in the room, the Civil War, or the War Between the States, was just another history lesson. Sure, we all knew some veterans, and we had all learned about the war in school, but the war was not real to us. We were not there, and there was no way we could even imagine what these two veterans had been through.

My mother had a strange way of knowing how to say and do things at just the right time. From the kitchen she appeared with something under a white towel. She set it down in front of Dr. MacNamarra. From a small serving table just behind MacNamarra she set some dessert plates and forks beside what was covered by the towel. Professor MacNamarra pulled back the towel and there was a peach pie. Dr. MacNamarra stood and looked across the table at Summerhill. Neither said a word, nor did anyone else.

MacNamarra picked up a small serving knife in his left hand and steadied the pie plate with a weak right arm that he could barely control. No one in the room spoke, or even moved. We just watched as he cut a piece of the pie, put it on one of the small plates, and laid a fork beside it. With his left arm he pushed the plate slowly across the table toward Mr. Summerhill, who sat silently staring at an imaginary spot on the table. The Confederate veteran did not know what to say or do. My mother had tears in her eyes, and I guess most of the rest of us did, too. The professor then cut himself a piece and sat back down to eat it.

Everyone disappeared, including Daddy. These two men deserved to be alone. I lingered on the steps a bit, really taken by what I had just seen. Summerhill and MacNamarra ate in silence. It was kind of like watching Lee surrender to Grant at Appomattox Court House, when the Civil War was over.

When they were done, they walked out onto the side porch. Daddy must have thought I was going to follow them, because he opened the kitchen door just enough to catch my attention, shook his head and silently said, "No."

I know for a fact they talked way late into the night. Their voices were quiet so we had no idea what they talked about. I've always tried to imagine, but I guess it really does not matter. That was their time and their conversation.

Check out time at the Inn was 12:00 noon, but on that July morning, everyone departed well before 7:00. The festivities in Gettysburg were scheduled to begin at 9:00 a.m. sharp, and the ride from the Inn would take at least an hour and a half. All of our guests were on their way to Gettysburg. Daddy had promised to take us to Gettysburg for the day.

Dr. MacNamarra and Mr. Summerhill were up and had coffee early. Even though they had checked out, they were still chatting on the side porch. And just like the previous night, we could not make out what they were saying.

After I had my breakfast, I left the kitchen and walked up toward the desk. My mother stopped me and told me not to bother the men. I was the curious type, and I guess my folks thought I might start asking questions or something. My mother also said we should not hurry them along, because there was enough going on in Gettysburg, that it would not matter if we got there a bit late.

I walked up to the registration desk and checked the book to make sure everyone had checked out. Tinasia had come down from her house, because she was going to ride with us. We both stood by the desk. I whispered to her not to say anything. She gave me one of those "Why?" looks, and I told her I would explain later.

I could hear a little of what MacNamarra and Summerhill were saying, and my curiosity really had the better of me.

"I'm sorry for what happened last night, I guess I ruined this reunion for both of us," Summerhill said.

"No, not for me. You've been carrying more than that minie ball around for the past fifty years," Dr. MacNamarra said to Summerhill. "You finally got a lot of hurt, pain, and hatred off your chest. All in all, that bullet you've been carrying has really gotten heavy over the past fifty years. Maybe if the war had ended differently, you would have felt different," MacNamarra said.

"Maybe, I don't know, and right now I really don't care anymore. I'm gonna do something I should have done years ago." Summerhill reached into his pocket, took one last look at the minie ball still marked from where it hit the bone in his leg, and threw it down into the woods beside the Inn. He turned to Dr. MacNamarra, reached down and took his weak right hand and shook it gently.

MacNamarra said nothing, but instead just nodded to Summerhill. As both men headed toward their cars, I could not help but look toward the woods where Summerhill had thrown the bullet that had hit him. I made a quick mental picture of the area where I thought it landed. Later, after many hours of searching, I retrieved the bullet and I still have it.

Looking back, I heard the professor ask Summerhill if he would see him in Gettysburg. "Nope, no, you won't. I'm headed for home. I had my reunion right here." They shook hands again before getting in their cars. As Summerhill headed west back down Route 30, Professor MacNamarra drove east toward Gettysburg.

Daddy had been watching too, from the back of the dining room. Walking toward the desk, he said to Tinasia and me, "There'll be lots of stories told in Gettysburg over the next few days, but none of them will match what we just saw."

Later that day, we went into Gettysburg. It was a great day, and it was well past midnight until we got back to the Inn. But like Daddy had said, there was nothing in Gettysburg to match the reunion we had seen at the Inn.

We never heard of Mr. Summerhill again, but many years later we heard about Dr. MacNamarra. Guests from State College left a newspaper from their town on one of the rockers on the side porch. As I picked it up to throw it away, I noticed the headline: "Pennsylvania's Last Gettysburg Veteran Dies." The picture just under the headline looked familiar to me. The brief article read as follows:

A retired professor of history, Dr. Robert D. MacNamarra, died yesterday at his home. Dr. MacNamarra was born in McAllesterville in Juniata County. He served with the 151st Pennsylvania Infantry during the Civil War. He was wounded during the Battle of Gettysburg. Dr. MacNamarra had been a member of the history department at Pennsylvania State University in State College from 1870 until his retirement in 1912. He had risen to the rank of a full professor, and following his retirement was named professor emeritus. Prior to his death, Dr. MacNamarra was Pennsylvania's oldest living Civil War veteran to have fought in the Battle of Gettysburg. He was 107.

4

Poison Ivy

Behind the Lincoln Inn, there is a flat area surrounded by a stand of beautiful big pine trees. This area used to be covered with brush, some small trees, and a lot of vines. We never played in there much when we were kids, because we knew some of the vines were poison ivy. We weren't really good at knowing the difference between poison ivy and other kinds of vines, so we just stayed out of there.

During the summer of 1909, Daddy decided it was time to clear this area and make it part of the large lawn behind the Inn. We did not have air conditioning back then, so on hot summer nights we spent as much time as possible outdoors. Our guests enjoyed the picnic tables and swings we had on the lawn behind the Inn. Each spring it was my job to scrape, sand, and repaint them. We mostly painted them white, except for two years. In 1926 and again in 1976, we added a little red and blue to the white. Those years marked the 150th and the 200th birthday of the Declaration of Independence. I did the painting for both of those special years.

If you have never had poison ivy, you have no idea how miserable it can make you feel. You itch, so you scratch, then your skin stings and burns. The stinging and burning make you itchy, so you scratch again and the cycle continues. It can go on and on like that until you are completely miserable. Some people don't get poison ivy. I always thought they were very lucky. If you are allergic to poison ivy, and most folks I know are, you can also swell up where it touches you.

Almost everyone I have ever met has a cure for poison ivy. One cure works just about as well as the others, and that's not very well. When we worked around poison ivy, we were always careful. If we touched it, we washed ourselves with some of Mama's laundry soap. If the ivy touched our clothes, Mama washed them separately from the other clothes.

Daddy and I started clearing the back of the lawn early on a mid-July morning. I can't remember the exact date, but I know it was close to his birthday and that was July 14. We figured it would take us just a few hours, but once we got started, we ran into some larger brush than Daddy had counted on. There was poison ivy everywhere, too. Dad said, "The poison ivy couldn't be any thicker in here if we had planted it!" Daddy knew we would hit some ivy, so we dressed with long sleeves and long pants that we tucked into our boots. We wore gloves and hats to help keep the shiny poison ivy leaves away from our bare skin.

The lawn, or the meadow as Mom called it, was shaded most of the day, but it was still hot during the heat of summer. A narrow stream ran down the side of the mountain, and there was a small pool just behind the flat area we were clearing. The little pool was shallow, only six or eight inches deep, but Grace and I loved to splash around in it when it was hot.

During most of the year the stream ran, but if the summer was really hot and there was not much rain, it would slow to a trickle. Daddy did not think the stream was a reliable source of water for the Inn, so he and Mr. Graffenburg built a stone spring house on the edge of the meadow, on the west side of the Inn. This spring house was fed by a small natural spring. Water that ran off the roof of the Inn when it rained was piped into the spring house too.

By noon we had most of the brush cleared out. Grace brought lunch out to Dad and me, after she and Mom fed the guests. I can even remember what we had. Mom sent us some pieces of cold fried chicken and some biscuits left over from supper the night before. Grace brought us a jar of water right from the spring house. We sat on a log from one of the trees we cut down. "After lunch we'll pile the brush and burn it," Daddy said as we started eating.

Mom walked out to check on us, just as we were finishing lunch. "Did you have enough to eat?" she said as she walked toward us.

"Sure, plenty," Daddy replied.

"We're almost done Mom," I added.

"It looks good! The guests will be able to walk back and see the stream if they want to," Mama said.

"As hot and dry as it's been, I'm surprised it's still running," Dad said, as he got up and pulled his gloves back on. I knew that was my sign to get ready to start working again too. My dad was a tireless worker. When he set his mind to a job, he stuck with it until it was done and done right. That's my way of working too.

The clearing we made looked good. I figured that by next spring I'd have another swing and a picnic table or two more to paint. Daddy was busy piling up the brush we had cut. We made a pile on the edge of the clearing. When we were done, my dad told me to go inside and wash up really well. He reminded me to use lots of soap just in case any of the ivy touched my skin.

As I headed for the house, I could hear the sharp crackling of the fire he had started in order to burn the brush pile. He stayed by the fire, using a rake to keep the brush together as it burned. The smoke was thick at first, but as the fire slowly died down, all that was left were some charred vines and glowing coals from the logs and branches that had been burned. After an hour or so, all that remained were some ashes.

After I had cleaned up a bit, I went out onto the east porch of the Inn to read a little. Daddy was sitting on one of the white rockers. He looked at me and did not say a word. Something didn't look right. He was all red and his face was swelled up. I said, "Are you okay, Dad?"

"I must . . . I must have . . ., breathed in too much smoke," he finally said, very much out of breath. He tried to sit forward in the chair but he could not. Settling back, he said in a voice just above a whisper, "Go get your mother, Mac." I knew there was something wrong, so I hurried into the kitchen to find Mama.

By the time we got back to him, his face was even redder and his lips were turning blue. His breathing was very heavy, and he was working hard for every breath. "I'll call Buc," Mama said as she ran back into the Inn. "Mac, stay with your father," she told me. I looked at my dad and he winked at me. I was only fifteen at the time, but I was not stupid. I knew my dad was in big trouble. After she called, Mama came back out onto the porch and sat beside Daddy. She told me to go and get some rags and cold water. She rubbed Daddy's face with them. He nodded to her that it felt good.

A small-framed older lady had just checked in with two other women who were much younger. They had missed lunch so Mother had set them up with some tea and butter cookies in the dining room. The older of the three women came out onto the porch and walked right over to my dad. In a quiet voice she said, "Has he been around burning brush?" Somewhat shocked by the question, my mother just looked at her.

"We were burning brush behind the Inn most of the morning and afternoon," I said.

"My guess is that there was some poison in the brush and this time of year it's dangerous to burn it. The oil in the ivy is carried by the smoke and it's like rubbing it all over yourself. If you breath it, you can actually get it in your lung." My mother kept rubbing my dad's face with the cool water. He never moved. My mother never responded to what the older lady said.

"If there's water around anywhere, our best bet is to get him in it as soon as possible. I saw this last year in Texas after the floods. When they burned the rubbish left behind after the waters went down, lots of guys ended up like this. Sorry to say, some of them died."

It only took Buc about fifteen minutes to make it up the mountain. We were lucky he was not busy that day. As he walked through the double front doors he said, "Grace where's your daddy?"

"Out on the porch," Grace said. She was only twelve at the time, but she knew Daddy was sick, really sick.

"Francis, what's the problem here," Dr. Buckman said as he knelt down in front of Daddy's chair. Dad just shook his head from side to side, as he rested it on the back of the rocker. His face was now even bigger and redder. His eyes were almost swelled shut. He looked horrible. The elder lady, who wore a black dress, stood back so she would not be in the way.

Buc knew Daddy was not going to be able to talk, so he asked Mama, "Arlene, what was he doing when this happened?"

"He and Mac had cleared some brush back in the meadow," Mom replied in a very nervous voice.

"He smells of smoke," Buc said.

"Well, after they had the area cleared, he burned the brush."

"I want to listen to your heart, Francis," Buc said as he unbuttoned Daddy's flannel shirt. Everyone was quiet while Buc listened. "Heart sounds good, but his lungs sound real congested," Buc said. Buc stood up and looked at Daddy's face. His eyes were closed, so Buc shook him a bit and said, "Francis, did you breathe some smoke from the fire?" Daddy did not answer. Buc turned to me and asked if there was any poison ivy in the brush we had cleared. I said I thought there was.

My mother looked at the lady in the black dress and said, "How did you know that?" It was obvious my mother was so scared she either didn't hear or didn't remember what the lady in the black dress had said.

"Like I said, I saw this last year several times when I was in Texas after their big floods."

"I can't say for sure, but that's my best guess too," Buc said. "What did they do for the guys in Texas?" He looked at the lady in the black dress.

"We put them in cold water, or at least as cold as we could find. That was all we could do to keep the swelling from killing them."

Mama said, "You kids go inside."

"No point in that Arlene, they already know their daddy is sick," Buc said.

Buc, Mom, Grace and I carried my dad to the stream. The lady in the black dress walked behind us. We carried him right in the chair he was sitting in. He was looking worse all the time. If I hadn't known it was my dad, I would never have recognized him. His breathing was very labored, and a few times I thought he had stopped breathing. The look on Dr. Buckman's face told me this was a real problem.

"Take his shirt, boots and socks off," Buc said to my mother. While she was doing that, Buc took off his own shoes and socks, and rolled his pant legs up to his knees. "Okay, now we've got to get him in the water." In a louder voice Buc said to Dad, "Francis, we're putting you in the water, it's gonna be cold, but it should help your breathing." Daddy couldn't even answer.

"Arlene, you and I'll have to lock arms to get him out of the chair. Mac, you grab your dad's legs and Grace, you hold his head." Grace started to cry when she looked down at Daddy. "There's no time for that Honey. Your daddy's gonna be okay. You just hold his head still," Buc said as we lifted Dad out of the white rocking chair from the side porch of the Inn.

Buc had moved a big stone toward one edge of the little stream. There was about a foot of water in the small pool we laid my dad in. Mama folded Daddy's shirt over and put it on the stone to make a pillow. Daddy groaned and said, "The water . . . the water feels good."

"That's good Francis, just relax," Buc said as he laid his stethoscope on Dad's chest. It looked like Dad went to sleep. Buc looked up at Mama and said, "At least he's no worse. Now all we can do is wait." Buc moved the chair that we carried Daddy in right to the edge of the little stream. He undid the black bow tie around his neck, unbuttoned his vest, and eased himself into the chair.

The older lady in the black dress walked slowly to the edge of the little stream and looked at Daddy. She said, "You'll know in just a few hours or so. The ones who made it when we were in Texas seemed to hold their own right along. The ones who didn't make it got worse really quick. This fellow isn't out of the woods yet, but it doesn't look like he's getting any worse."

Grace walked up behind Mom and peeked around to look at Daddy lying in the stream. He didn't look much better, but he wasn't making so much noise when he breathed. Just about that time, Mr. and Mrs. Graffenburg came around the side of the Inn.

"Arlene, what can we do?" Mr. Graffenburg asked very abruptly. He didn't even waste time asking what was wrong. He just knew someone was in trouble and he wanted to help. He had seen Buc hurrying into the Inn and he knew something was wrong. Buc was not usually a hurrying kind of fellow. Normally he had two speeds, slow – and even slower.

Before Mama could answer, Buc said, "Nothing to do Andy – your buddy's got a dose of poison ivy in his lungs. All we can do is keep him cool and hope the swelling doesn't shut off his breathing." Mr. Graffenburg walked over and looked at Daddy laying in the stream. He put his hands on his hips and just shook his head.

"Can't we take him somewhere to get some help?" Mr. Graffenburg asked.

Buc stood up and walked over to where Mr. Graffenburg was standing. "Andy, if there was anything that could be done, don't you think I'd be doing it?" Buc snapped. Dr. Buckman never snapped at folks when he talked. I knew he was as worried as the rest of us.

"Sorry Buc. It's just that when a friend is in trouble you try to help them."

"I know Andy. I'm in the business of helping folks. But like I said, there's nothing to do now but wait. His heart sounds okay, and his lungs are still congested, but I don't think he's getting any worse. We're just gonna have to be patient."

Like she knew they were friends, the lady in the black dress said, "Your friend will be okay if we can keep him cool."

Mr. Graffenburg realized he could not do anything to help my dad in his present condition, but he had to do something. "Arlene, Millie and I'll stay here with you to help through supper, and the kids can stay with us through the night."

"Oh, we do have some guests, and they'll be expecting supper," Mom replied.

"Just let me take care of things, Arlene," Mrs. Graffenburg said, already walking toward the Inn.

"It may not be as good, but we can make do," Mr. Graffenburg added as he joined his wife. The lady in the black dress didn't say anything, but she too walked back to the Inn.

Mama called after them, "I've got everything started and most of it's on the stove." Buc went up on the porch and came back with a chair for Mom. Daddy had drifted a little in the water, and Buc asked me to pile a few stones close to Daddy so he would not turn over.

"The last thing we need is for him to take in any water. It would surely kill him."

That's when it hit me. No one had said it even though I guess we all thought about it. Daddy could die. When I realized that, I started to cry. Buc saw me and took my arm. He pulled me a little closer to him, and he said, "Grace, you come here too. Now look, for right now your daddy is okay. He's not good, but he is okay. Like the lady in the black dress said, the best thing is that he's not getting any worse. And the last thing he needs is to see any of us crying. We're gonna do all we can, and we just have to wait. Daddy needs rest, and you two need to eat."

Mr. & Mrs. Graffenburg had already started serving the guests, and Mama got a plate ready for Grace and me. She didn't eat, but instead she went out back with Dad and Buc. After the guests were served and the tables were cleared, Mrs. Graffenburg sat with Grace and me for awhile. Mr. Graffenburg went outside. Mrs. Graffenburg kept telling us that Daddy was going to be okay. I think she was trying to convince herself too.

"Get me a cup, quick, Millie! We need some ice," Mr. Graffenburg said rushing into the kitchen. I stood up and he snapped at me, "No, you kids stay here!"

"Is Francis okay?" Mrs. Graffenburg asked, holding both hands to the sides of her face.

"I think so. Buc says he needs a drink." Mr. Graffenburg grabbed a small piece of ice from the icebox and he was back out the door as quickly as he had come in.

"Mr. Graffenburg didn't mean to holler at you, Mac. He's just worried about your daddy."

"I know," I said, sitting back down.

Mrs. Graffenburg hugged Grace, and again she told us that Daddy would be fine. I finished a small piece of cherry pie and put my dish in the sink. I walked into our living room and looked out the large window. Buc and Mr. Graffenburg were holding my dad up in a sitting position. The lady in the black dress was kneeling in the water in front of him, holding a cup to his mouth. It looked to me like he was drinking some of the water. I thought that was good. Mama was holding his hand and she kissed him on the forehead just as Buc and Mr. Graffenburg laid him back down into the water.

Mama came back into the Inn, and she told Mrs. Graffenburg that he was no worse. "Dr. Buckman said his breathing is a little better, but he's still in trouble. The lady in the black dress seems to think it's a really good sign that he's not getting any worse." The two friends of the lady in the black dress were also out back by the stream. The other guests knew there was nothing they could do, so they sat on the side porch. The Inn was usually a happy place, but that night it was somber.

Nothing changed much through the evening, and soon Mama told us it was time for bed. Mr. and Mrs. Graffenburg wanted to take us to their house, but Grace and I wanted to stay home.

I wanted to do something to help, but I didn't know what I could do. It was going to be a long night, and I did not feel right about just going to bed. I wanted to be there if Daddy needed me. Then I had an idea. I went down to the basement and found a long piece of string. I hoped it would be long enough to stretch from the Inn back to the creek, and it was.

Mom had some small trinkets sitting around on a shelf near the back of the Inn. One of the trinkets was a small brass bell in the shape of an apple. I didn't think she would mind so I took the bell and tied one end of the string to it. I tied a loop of the string around the post of my bed, and I dropped the rest of the string out the window. Then I took the other end back and tied it to a tree right beside where Buc and Mr. Graffenburg were sitting with Daddy.

"What are you doing Mac?" Buc asked.

"The other end of this string is tied to a bell beside my bed. If you need me during the night, just pull on this string and I'll come right out," I told him.

"Mac, you're just like your dad," Mr. Graffenburg said. "When someone's in trouble, you want to help."

"It's a deal Mac," Buc said. "If we need you, we'll ring the bell. And if we can get this swelling reversed through the night, we'll ring it too."

I was standing near the lady in the black dress. She turned to me, smiled and gave me a hug. I was just a kid and I was as tall as she was. In a soft voice she said, "You need some sleep, young man. Your daddy is going to pull through this. I just know it." There was something about her that was comforting. I believed her.

"Thanks," is all I said. I took another look at my dad, sleeping in the small pool of water and I headed back into the Inn.

It had been a long day, and I was exhausted. Before I fell asleep, though, I took another look out my window. Dr. Buckman, Mr. Graffenburg, my mom and the lady in the black dress were just silhouettes sitting beside the little stream. There was a small kerosene lantern sitting beside them that gave off a golden glow. The sound of cicadas chirping was the last sound I heard.

The next morning, a familiar whistle startled me awake. I had heard it many times before, and I could almost whistle like that myself. The only guy I knew who could whistle like that was my dad. I jumped out of my bed and looked out back. My dad, who looked like himself again, was standing in the middle of the yard with a blanket draped over his shoulders. His thick black hair was still wet and his pants had not even begun to dry.

Dr. Buckman and Mr. Graffenburg were sitting at one of the picnic tables having a cup of coffee. The lady in the black dress was sitting there too. My dad whistled again and smiled, as he motioned with his hand for me to come down. Just at that moment, the whole thing just sort of crashed down on me, when I considered again just how easily my dad could have died.

When I pulled myself together, I put my clothes on quickly and went out back. Dr. Buckman was getting ready to leave and Mr. Graffenburg had already gone. Dad looked a little washed out, but he certainly looked better than he did when we carried him back to the stream.

"Hey, we all learned a lesson, Francis. No more burning poison ivy," Buc said. "I think you're fine, but a couple of days taking it easy wouldn't hurt anything."

"Thanks Buc. See Arlene and she'll pay you," Dad said.

"Nah, the Mrs. and I'll just be up Sunday for dinner. I'll want to check on you," Dr. Buckman said as he pushed his pant legs down and put his socks and shoes on.

My mother came out of the Inn carrying a glass of milk and two pieces of jelly toast for me. "Hungry?" she said with a smile.

"Yes," I replied, hugging her around the waist.

Daddy sat down across from me and said, "I just couldn't bring myself to ring that bell, Mac. I figured if I whistled at you, you would know it was me, and you would know I was okay. I thought the bell might scare you."

The lady in the black dress just smiled at my dad and me. She seemed to be enjoying our conversation. Daddy looked at her and said, "Mac, I'm sure you don't know who our special guest is." The elderly lady in the black dress blushed and smiled. "Mac, this is

Miss Clara Barton, the founder of the American Red Cross." I knew who Clara Barton was. She was one of the first people in Washington to go out to help the Union soldiers wounded at the first Battle of Bull Run, and she decided right then to dedicate the rest of her life to helping people in need.

My mother was standing behind Miss Barton when she said, "She has something to show you that is really beautiful and very special." From her pocket she took out a small purple jewelry box. She opened it and inside was a broach with two large diamonds and a big sapphire mounted on it. The broach was half silver and half gold.

"The good people of Johnstown gave this to me in October 1889, after their flood. That was the first really big disaster that my Red Cross had to face, and we did a great job helping the people get back on their feet. I always like to say we were the first to arrive, and the last to leave."

She rubbed her one finger over the broach and shook her head, like she was remembering something. She looked at me and said, "More than 2,200 people died in that flood. It was just awful. Water can cause a lot of damage and even kill people. But just look at your daddy. Water saved his life."

As she sipped a cup of tea she talked to us about the work she and the Red Cross had done since the Civil War. She told us that she was going back to Glen Echo in Maryland to retire. She had been back to Johnstown earlier in the week for a visit and she had taken her Johnstown broach along to wear to a dinner being held in her honor.

Miss Barton and her two friends left before lunch. They wanted to make it back to Glen Echo before dark. In the guest book, Mother drew a small red cross in the margin next to Miss Clara Barton's name. She told me how happy she was that in our time of need, Miss Barton was there to help.

Later that day, I untied the bell from the side of my bed and I rolled up the string. The bell was a scary thing when I looked at it. If it had rung through the night, it could have meant that my dad was worse or maybe he had died. I decided I never wanted to hear that bell ring again, so I took the ringer out.

We still have the silent bell, and it sits on the same shelf where I found it during the summer of 1909. I never did put the ringer back in. Even since, it's been just a silent little trophy to my dad, my mom, Dr. Buckman, the Graffenburgs, and the kind, older lady in the black dress.

5

German Spies

By the summer of 1918, American "Doughboys" had been in Europe for a little more than a year. My dad had become the local expert on the war. He got his daily updates through the newspapers, and even though the news was a little old by the time he got it, it was still news to us. World War I, the Great War, was the biggest news story of the day. It seemed it was all folks could talk about.

Daddy was always patriotic, but during both of the world wars his patriotism became almost fanatic. There was a small wooden figure of Uncle Sam that stood on the registration desk in the lobby. It had been there for years. During the war it became all but sacred to him. For my dad, that simple red, white and blue wooden figure was the very personification of General Pershing's Expeditionary Forces in Europe. It stood for everything that was good about America.

World War I started in 1914 and lasted until 1918. It ended with an armistice signed on the eleventh hour, of the eleventh day, of the eleventh month of that year. By the time it was over more than 30 nations had been involved, with great suffering and loss of life.

For the first few years, the United States tried to remain neutral. The Germans were threatening American merchant ships and passenger ships on the high seas, and they had even sunk a few. When the *Lusitania* was sunk in May 1915 by a German U-boat off the coast of Ireland, 124 Americans perished. There was a loud outcry in this country. Americans turned against the Germans, and folks worried about German sabotage and espionage in this country. The government warned against talking in public about things that might help the Germans and their allies. A common warning of the day was, "The slip of a lip could sink a ship!" Everyone was concerned about spies for the Kaiser's Germany.

President Woodrow Wilson's plan to keep us out of the war worked for a while, but on April 2, 1917, he had to ask Congress to declare war on Germany and their major ally, Austria-Hungary. The United States was at war!

In June 1917, units of the American Expeditionary Forces, led by General John J. "Black Jack" Pershing landed in France. By the end of the fighting in November 1918, more than 2,000,000 Americans had served in the A.E.F. Soldiers who fought in World War I were nicknamed "Doughboys," a nickname for U.S. soldiers that goes back to the Civil War. They got the name because the buttons on their uniforms looked like flour dumplings, called doughboys, that were cooked in soup. When the Americans first got to Europe, they were called "Teddies" or "Sammies." They didn't like either of those names, so the soldiers suggested "doughboys," and the nickname just stuck.

During the summer of 1918, I was between my sophomore and junior year at Millersville Normal School and I was working at the Inn. I had already decided that after graduation, in the spring of 1920, I was going to enlist in the Navy.

We were aware of the war, but the actual fighting was still thousands of miles away. Then, on a rather warm afternoon in August 1918, one of our guests had an accidental encounter with Dad's Uncle Sam figure. It almost resulted in an international incident.

When he walked into our lobby, he looked more tired than a man should be at two o'clock in the afternoon. His suitcase was small and worn. His light-colored suit looked tired, too. His tie was loose and the top button of his starched white shirt was undone. His coat was draped over his left arm, and he carried his suitcase in his right hand. The heels of his shoes scraped the floor lightly as he approached the front desk. The beads of sweat on his forehead reminded me just how hot it was.

"Do you have a room for the night?" the man asked with a heavy German accent.

From behind the counter my mother said, "Yes we do, sir, and a good dinner too!"

My dad was back in the kitchen, but when he heard the accent of the guest, he sat his coffee mug down and walked out to the desk. Daddy just looked at him for awhile. Then he turned the registration book around and moved it toward the guest so he could sign. Daddy asked, "Where are you from Mr. ----?" pausing to allow the tired-looking man with a German accent time to give his name.

"Gubenmayer. Oscar Gubenmayer is my name and I'm from Baltimore, Maryland."

Daddy's initial thoughts were confirmed. The name and the accent were definitely German, and Daddy wanted more information. "What line of work are you in, Mr. Gubenmayer?"

"Salesman," he replied, and without pausing he asked my mother, "What room will I be in, please?"

"Room three, top of the stairs and to the right, " Mom replied, pointing to the stairs. "We'll be eating at 5:30 and we're having ham, cabbage and potatoes. Hope you like that."

"Will be just fine," Gubenmayer replied in a voice that was growing more tired by the minute.

Mr. Gubenmayer turned the registration book around and slid it back across the counter. As he did, the corner of the book hit the Uncle Sam figure and knocked it off the counter. Before Daddy or Mr. Gubenmayer could grab it, it crashed to the floor.

"I am so sorry, Sir," Gubenmayer said.

Daddy offered no response in words, but if looks could kill, there would have been one dead German salesman from Baltimore in our lobby.

"Is it broken?" Mr. Gubenmayer asked.

Dad did not answer. He just looked right at Gubenmayer, set the figure back on the counter, and walked back into the kitchen.

"Again, I am so sorry! I meant no harm at all. It is a beautiful figure of Uncle Sam." Mr. Gubenmayer picked up his suitcase and headed up the stairs.

I was sitting at the kitchen table when my dad came back into the kitchen. Mom was right behind him. "Francis, you were more than a little rude to Mr. Gubenmayer," mother said in a whispered voice.

Daddy offered no reply. He picked up his coffee mug and took a drink. "I don't think he knocked Uncle Sam off the counter on purpose, do you?" Mom asked.

"Maybe not," Dad replied. Dad was angry and there was no point in pushing him. He had something else to say and we were just going to have to wait. "The government thinks there may be Germans in this country who are spying on us. Last time I was in McConnellsburg I saw a notice in the post office, and I've seen several notices in the papers."

"Do you think . . . ?" My mother could not even finish her sentence.

"I don't know Arlene," Dad said in a whispered voice. "But I can't lie, the thought is on my mind. When he knocked Sam off the counter, he might just as well have taken a shot right at General Pershing, and I don't care if he did it on purpose or not!"

"Go on Francis," Mother said, forcing a smile. "He said he's a salesman from Baltimore."

"Arlene," Dad said, pausing and looking right at her. "What do you think he's gonna do, introduce himself as Mr. Oscar Gubenschmidt, or Gubenstine or whatever, German spy?"

Mother's expression changed dramatically when she asked, "What do you think we should do?"

At this point, I offered my opinion. "Well, we don't know anything for sure. For all we know he's just another guest with a German accent and a German sounding name. He probably is a salesman from Baltimore." Based on two bits of information, our suspicions and imaginations were running at full speed.

Throughout the afternoon six other guests checked in. The closer it got to dinner, the more obvious the main course became. The smell of ham, cabbage and potatoes filled the lobby. By 5:30 the guests had gathered, all but one. Mr. Gubenmayer was still in his room. There had not been a sound from that room.

Mama was looking out the kitchen door, when Dad came up behind her and asked, "What about the German?"

"Francis, that's enough. The man has a name. You talk about him like he's not even a person." Dad made no response.

I walked past my folks and said, "I'll go get him." Just as I reached the top of the stairs, Mr. Gubenmayer came out of room three and shut the door behind him.

"How are you, young man?" he asked me.

"Fine sir," I replied. "Did you get some rest?"

"Yes I did!"

Mr. Gubenmayer and I walked down the steps together. He looked a bit more rested. "I have a spot for you fellows right here," my mother said. She was carrying a large bowl of applesauce so she nodded toward two chairs at the head of the table. Dad and the other guests were already seated.

"This smells wonderful," Mr. Gubenmayer said as he took his seat. I took the seat between him and my father. I thought it best if someone was between them.

Supper was quiet that night, and that was rare. Dad always tried to engage the guests in conversation. He was curious about them, and he often asked questions. Sometimes my mother would scold him later, saying the guests might think he was being noisy. Dad would always say, "No, not being noisy, just being friendly!"

This night, however, things were quiet. If Mr. Gubenmayer was in fact a German spy, he was not going to get a bit of information from Francis McGettegen. Gubenmayer tried to talk with me. He asked what I was doing. I told him I was in college and home for the summer. Dad looked at me and I knew he was not happy that I was talking with him. Mr. Gubenmayer must have picked up on the tension. He finished his meal quickly. Mama offered him seconds and he declined. By 6:00 he was back in his room.

My sister Grace and Tinasia had been in McConnellsburg most of the day. They were at the Buckman's, planning a party to announce Grace's engagement to George A. Buckman. George attended medical school in Philadelphia, and would graduate with the class of 1920. He was Buc's only son.

Tinasia and Grace had known each other all their lives. Grace was the maid of honor at our wedding, and Tinasia served the same role for her and George. "The party will be lovely, Mac," Tinasia said as she kissed me on the forehead. I was perched in one of the large white chairs near the front of the main room of the Inn.

"I'm sure it will be," I said getting up from the chair. I dropped my book on the chair, then followed her into the kitchen. "Am I invited?" I asked.

Grace laughed and said, "We're not sure yet. You'll just have to wait and see if you get an invitation.

"We had a little excitement here today," I said. I explained the incident between Dad and the German guest.

"Oh, Daddy is just foolin'," Grace said.

"I don't think so. He was serious, as serious as I've ever seen him." Tinasia asked me if I thought Mr. Gubenmayer might really be a spy. I replied that since I had never met a spy before, I really couldn't say. I told my wife and my sister that Mr. Oscar Gubenmayer from Baltimore, Maryland, just looked like a tired salesman who needed a good meal and some sleep.

Tinasia said, "Even if he is a spy, what kind of information is he gonna get around here?"

"Hey, maybe he's looking for a good recipe for ham, cabbage, and potatoes for the Kaiser's army," I added. "If he hadn't knocked old Sam off the desk, I don't think Dad would have thought much about him. That was what got the whole thing started. Dad's heard about the possibility of spies being here in the United States, and maybe he's just thinking too much about it."

We did not talk any more about the spy that evening, since Dad had turned in early. Mama joined us in the kitchen and she never mentioned Gubenmayer at all. Years later she told me she was just too scared to talk about the possibility.

Gracie's engagement party seemed much more interesting, so that is what we talked about. Mama recalled when she and Dad got engaged. I always liked hearing her tell stories because she had a remarkable memory. She offered so much detail, you could almost picture what she was talking about. She could describe who she was with, what they ate, what they wore, and if pushed, what color socks the mailman was wearing that date.

Grace, Tinasia, and Mama went off to bed. I was the last one to turn in, and before I did, I took a quick stroll around the Inn. Dad and I had an unwritten agreement that the last one up at night checked the place before turning in. When I got to the top of the main steps, I noticed a light under the bottom of the door of room three. I could not hear anything, but Mr. Gubenmayer was up. "He's probably in there right now planning how to take Washington himself," I thought. Just as quickly, I laughed and shook my head, having amused myself just a little. Quietly, I headed back down the stairs and went to bed.

Dad rose early the next morning and so did Mr. Gubenmayer. When I got up, I went into the kitchen, where Mama and Tinasia were busy getting breakfast ready. There were two sets of dirty dishes in the sink.

Mama saw me looking at the dishes in the sink and she explained, "Dad and Mr. Gubenmayer have been up for awhile, so they had an early breakfast. Mr. Gubenmayer asked to make a phone call before they ate. Ever since, they've been talking." I looked into the lobby and they were both leaning on the front desk. Dad was on one side and Mr. Gubenmayer was on the other. "They have been there for more than an hour, just like that," Mama whispered over my shoulder. I couldn't hear anything, but judging from their expressions, things were much better between them than they had been yesterday.

Finally, Mr. Gubenmayer reached across the desk and shook Dad's hand. I could faintly hear Dad say, "I'm sorry." Gubenmayer shook his head accepting the apology, but made it clear that it was not necessary. The two men walked out through the front door, and I went out into the lobby to watch them.

They were still talking when Dad turned abruptly and trotted up the front steps of the Inn and back into the lobby. He grabbed the Uncle Sam figure from the front desk, and walked back out to Gubenmayer, who had gotten into his car. Dad handed the figure to Mr. Gubenmayer, said something to him, shook his hand, and Gubenmayer drove off. With both hands in his pockets and his head down, Dad came back into the Inn.

"Hey, how are you this morning?" I said, not yet ready to ask anything about his conversation with our German guest.

"Get two cups of coffee, come out on the porch, and I'll tell you," Daddy said shaking his head as he went out onto the side porch. I did as he suggested. I wanted to hear this story.

I handed Dad his coffee and settled into one of the white rockers. He took a sip of coffee and started talking. "Mr. Oscar Gubenmayer is definitely not a German spy. He is a salesman, just like he said he was. He sells prescription medicines. He was born in Germany and moved to Baltimore with his parents when he was twelve. His wife, and his daughter and son live in Baltimore with him."

Dad took another sip of his coffee, set the cup back on the arm of the rocker and continued. "His son is an officer in the United States Navy. He graduated from the Naval Academy at Annapolis two years ago, and he has been in the Navy since. He was on board a British ship as an observer trying to determine the best route for the United States flotilla to cross the North Atlantic. The German U-boats, or submarines, have made it almost impossible to move through the waters of the North Atlantic."

"Well, last week the ship he was on, the *Glasgow*, did battle with a German ship named the *Dresden*, and even though both escaped, there were many casualties on both ships. An initial report listed Mr. Gubenmayer's son among the dead on board the *Glasgow*. A later report confirmed that he was still alive, but his condition was very serious. Mr. Gubenmayer was on the road in Pittsburgh, and each day he called his wife for word. It wasn't until this morning that they got the news they were waiting for."

Mama and Tinasia joined us on the porch and Dad briefly filled them in, then continued. "I was up early and as soon as he heard me in the lobby he came down to ask if he could use the phone. He found out that his son is being taken to Cape May, New Jersey. There is a huge hotel there, I think he said it's called the Admiral. Well, the Navy turned it into a hospital for soldiers and sailors brought back from the war. They can go to see him. He just has some broken bones and some burns on his left side."

Dad locked his fingers as he put his hands behind his head. "That's the first time I was ever rude to a guest. I told Oscar I was sorry." Daddy was feeling guilty and we all knew it.

"Dad, there is no way you could have known. The war has us all a little on edge," Tinasia said.

"Yes, but I was wrong. He needed a friend, not someone trying to make him out to be a spy," Dad said.

"Well, you made it right Francis," mother added.

"I know. I guess it was when he knocked Sam off the counter." Dad paused and we all respected his silence. "I gave him Uncle Sam. I asked him to give it to his son." Dad picked up his coffee cup and walked toward the kitchen. Mama just looked at Tinasia and me and smiled. We were all moved by what had happened and there was nothing to say.

We continued talking about the war until the fighting stopped in November, but we did not mention Gubenmayer or his son again. The experience had been difficult for my dad. One April afternoon in 1926, the whole incident came back to visit us.

A young couple came into the lobby. The man asked to speak to Mr. McGettegen. Tinasia was at the desk and she said, "Well, we have two Mr. McGettegens, and you're in luck, they're both here." Just then Daddy came in from the side porch, and offering his hand to the tall stranger he said, "I'm Francis McGettegen, may I help you?"

"Yes, I think you can, sir. I'm Robert Gubenmayer and this is my wife. My father . . ."

Without letting him finish, Dad said, ". . . is Oscar Gubenmayer. And you, young man, were wounded in World War I. You were on a British ship named the *Glasgow* when it happened."

"Yes sir, that's me exactly, and this is my wife Elizabeth."

"Arlene, come here quick!" Dad hollered toward the kitchen. I had come in from the side porch, and Dad made the necessary round of introductions.

"We're on our way to Erie," Elizabeth said. "Bob is going to work for Atlantic Oil Refining Company. He will be in charge of their Great Lakes Fleet."

Mama told everyone to sit down, and in no time she had lemonade and a plate of oatmeal raisin cookies on the big dining room table. We talked for more than two hours. For the first time, Dad revisited the initial meeting between him and Mr. Gubenmayer in 1918. He needed to do this, so he could finally put it behind him.

"Mr. McGettegen, you'll never know how much your kindness meant to my father. He said during the loneliest time in his life, you showed him kindness and took time to talk with him." My dad never said a word. He just looked down at his hands.

"When Bob's dad found out we were going to Erie, he insisted we stop and see you," Elizabeth added.

"Yes," Bob said, standing up and going toward the door, "He asked me to give you something." A moment later, he returned with Dad's wooden Uncle Sam figure in his hand. "I think this belongs to you, sir," he said, handing Sam back to Dad.

My dad was not an emotional man, but we knew he was at his limit. Mama filled the silence. "What a thoughtful thing for your father to do, Robert."

Without a word, Dad put Uncle Sam back on the counter where he had last stood during the summer of 1918. Turning to face the young couple, Dad said, "Thank your father for me, and let him know there is always a room for him here, and there will always be a place at my table for him."

"That goes for you folks, too," Mother added. "It's almost suppertime — can you stay?"

"I wish we could, Mrs. McGettegen, but I have to be in Erie by noon tomorrow, and even if we leave right now it's gonna be pushing it." As Dad walked them to the car, they continued chatting.

"Give your father my best, Robert."

"I will sir."

As the Gubenmayers pulled away Dad waved, then stood there silently until they were out of sight. This day had been long in coming for my father and it was a good one. A mistake for which he had a hard time forgiving himself was now behind him. He never said so, but I always believed he was relieved.

By the way, that red, white, and blue figure of Uncle Sam still stands on the front desk. I guess as long as Tinasia and I are here, it always will!

6

Mr. Ford's Model T

That October had started as a particularly warm one. As I recall the whole summer and early fall of 1924 was warmer than usual. Summers during the early 1920s were busy at the Inn. World War I was over and the Great Depression had not started yet, so times were prosperous. People seemed to be traveling more and more each year, and that was good for business.

We had a good routine around the Inn. Between Dad, Mom, Tinasia, and me, we were able to handle the Inn quite well. We each had certain things we were good at, and those were our chores. Looking back, I have to admit I had a good life at the Inn. I have always hoped that it was as good for Dad, Mom, and Tinasia.

We never had the chance to travel much, but there was always something we needed at the Inn, so we kept a car or two around. When we opened in 1894, Daddy had a team of horses and a large wagon. Because Mr. Graffenburg kept several horses for his lumber business, we usually kept our horses and wagon there. We even kept our car there for a time, because there was no place to keep it at the Inn.

Over the years, we have had a number of different cars around the Inn. My favorite was our 1924 Model T touring car. We had a 1916 Model T before that one, and we had a Model A after that. I cannot recall all the cars we have had at the Inn, but the '24 T is still my favorite. In fact, it's still in the garage under the Inn.

Because of the way the land slopes away from the east side of the Inn, we were able to put a garage under it, with enough room to fit two vehicles. Even though we have always kept a modern car, I've never gotten rid of the '24 T. I remember being so impressed with that car. We were proud of it in October 1924, when Dad and I first drove down to McConnellsburg. I am still proud of it today.

Our new car came with an instruction book and a repair manual. Dad and I both read them carefully. Up here on the mountain, you had to know how to take care of things when they needed to be fixed. The Model T was a good car for that. It was built so that if you could drive it, you could fix it too. It even came with its own tools. The toolbox was attached right to the side of the car. That made it handy. Daddy and I did all we could to get familiar with our new car, but one of our guests did more for us in that way than we could have ever done for ourselves. In fact, he is how we got the car to begin with.

As I said earlier, October 1924 was a particularly warm month, and we had a steady stream of travelers at the Inn. In early October, maybe around the 8th, two fellows came to the Inn sporting a 1924 Model T. When they arrived, they did not come directly into the Inn. Instead, they looked their car over real well. They checked everything from the tires up. They crawled under it, looked under the hood and even took the floorboards out to check the transmission. I watched them from inside the Inn. I was fascinated by how carefully they looked at their car.

I walked out onto the front porch and asked, "Is there anything wrong with her?"

"Not a thing," a crisp voice answered from underneath the car. "She's just fine. Took that mountain as easy as if she was running on the top of a table." After crawling out from under the car, the smaller of the two men walked toward me as he wiped his hands. He was still holding a long tool that he had used to check something under the car. "They just get better every year," he said, as though he had a real stake in the Ford Model T.

"We have a '16 and love her," I agreed.

"Dad's really proud of his cars," the younger man said.

"With good reason," I added. "Ford makes a great car."

"Nice to hear you say that," the older and smaller of the two men said. "I agree with you, but I guess that would come as no real surprise to anyone. After all . . . ." He didn't complete the sentence.

"What my dad means is, it should come as no real surprise to anyone that Henry Ford would think Ford Motor Company makes a good car."

"No, I guess not," I said, sticking my hand out. "I'm pleased to meet you, Mr. Ford. I'm Mac McGettegan."

"This is my son, Edsel. He and I are road testing one of our latest models. We had her to Atlantic City for a demonstration run, and I thought we'd drive her back to Dearborn instead of taking it back by train."

Both of the Fords were wearing long, tan-colored coats. When I shook Mr. Ford's hand I noticed that there was a monogram on the sleeve. It read, "HF" in a rounded script. When I shook the younger Mr. Ford's hand, his sleeve carried the monogram "EF." I learned later that the long coats they wore were called dusters. Since the Model T was driven in the open air, and since there were minor adjustments needed from time to time, the duster was a cover to keep the driver clean. Dusters were very common at that time, so the monograms helped folks to identify their duster. Each of the gentlemen was also wearing a driving cap that matched the duster

The older Mr. Ford was also wearing a pair of padded leather driving gloves. Older cars were not as easy to drive as cars are today, so a driver had to keep a really good grip on the wheel. And since there was no heater in the Model T, the leather gloves also kept the driver's hands warm in cold weather.

Edsel Ford said, "This is some mountain you folks live on."

"But we climbed her with no problem," the older Mr. Ford added.

My dad had walked out onto the porch, so I introduced him to the Fords. Dad was pleased to meet them, and the new Ford caught his eye immediately. "Not all that different from my '16 is she?" Dad asked in a rhetorical manner.

"Basics are the same, but a number of improvements have been added that we're really proud of at Ford," the older Mr. Ford said. "The T has been a great car since she was introduced in 1908, but that hasn't stopped us from doing everything we can be make it even better. Let me show you a few changes we've made over the years." Edsel had gone inside to register for the night. Henry, my dad, and I were busy going over the shiny new Ford.

Mr. Ford was not at all bashful about explaining his car to us. He covered every inch of it. It was clear that he not only owned the company, but he was also familiar with every phase of the company's operations right down to the smallest detail. He told us that the 1924, three door, open touring model had a retail price of $295.00. He said the deluxe model sold for $390.00. For the additional $95 dollars, you got a hand-operated windshield wiper, brass foot trays on the running boards, a side-mounted toolbox, and an electric starter. The 1924 model still had the hand crank starter on the front of the car as well.

When he picked up the hood he laughed a bit and asked if either of us could guess what the silver fixture on top of the third cylinder of the motor might be. I had no idea. My dad studied it for awhile. then said he thought it might be a type of whistle that operated off the compression of the motor. Mr. Ford said he was right. He explained that the National Audubon Society said they were afraid that as automobiles became more popular, all of the birds would be scared off by the sounds. Mr. Ford said that was nonsense, and to make his point, he developed a small whistle that could be attached to the car. It was operated from inside the car by way of a small wire that passed through the firewall into the engine compartment.

The car was built to seat five adults comfortably. It had wooden-spoked wheels, a convertible top that folded nicely behind the rear seat, and a rear-mounted spare tire. Mr. Ford explained that he and his engineers had developed a system of planetary gears that made steering the car a whole lot easier for folks. He said he wanted women to be able to drive Fords. On the dash there was just a single instrument and that was an amp meter. It indicated if the generator was working properly.

There were two other meters on the car as well. Atop the radiator there was a gull winged temperature gauge that warned when the water coolant in the engine was too hot. And on the side of the transmission, there was a clear glass tube in a brass case that told how much oil was in the engine. You could check the oil through this tube or you could turn a small valve to see if any oil dripped out. If it did, there was plenty of oil in the engine.

The younger Mr. Ford had checked himself and his father in for the night. Before the senior Mr. Ford would go inside, he asked if he could see our '16. Daddy took him around to the garage under the Inn. They were there some time. As they came into the Inn, they were talking cars like they were old friends. It was clear that they were enjoying each other's company.

That evening for dinner we had only the Fords as guests. Edsel had a rather light appetite, but his father ate more than enough for both of them. Mama had prepared baked chicken legs with a honey glaze, cooked carrots with a brown sugar sauce, oven baked lemon-pepper potatoes, slow-rise raisin and whole wheat bread, and a creamed cucumber salad. For dessert, she fixed deep-dish apple pie, topped with ice cream and spiced apple rings.

After we ate, Dad and Mr. Ford went back out with the new T. Edsel sat in the lobby reading the paper. I went outside with Daddy and Mr. Ford. He asked if we wanted to go for a drive, and of course we did. He gave Daddy and me each a turn to drive, and it was a real treat. It steered a good bit easier than our '16, and the motor seemed to have more power. As dusk approached, Mr. Ford lit the two kerosene running lights and told me to turn on the headlights. They were much improved over the lights on our '16. We drove almost to McConnellsburg before we turned around and headed back to the Inn.

When we returned, Tinasia had put out some coffee and cinnamon rolls hot from the oven. We sat around and talked late into the night. Edsel was a quiet man, just offering a comment or two from time to time. His father, on the other hand, was talkative and very interesting. We really enjoyed their visit and gained a whole new appreciation for the Model T and the growing automotive industry.

The next morning, Henry Ford and his son Edsel rose early, ate breakfast, and were on their way. They thanked us for our hospitality and were most generous in paying for their room. At first Dad protested, but Mr. Ford insisted, saying that he had sincerely enjoyed himself. As they drove away Dad said, "That's one great car."

I could tell from the way he spoke that he really liked that car. But our '16 was still in good shape, and Dad was not the type to get rid of something before its time was up. He pulled his T out of the garage later that day and gave it a good cleaning. I believe he had a whole new appreciation for it.

Well, as I've said before, we have had our share of surprises at the Lincoln Inn over the years, but Mr. Ford maybe gave us one of the most generous surprises we've ever received. There was no hiding the fact that Dad and I were both very impressed with the '24 Mr. Ford and his son were driving. It was also clear that Mr. Ford was pleased with how his car had performed on its run through the mountains of Pennsylvania. He had explained to us that one of the chief criticisms the T had received from its owners was that it had no power on mountains. The engineers at Ford had been working on that problem, and Mr. Ford was anxious to see just how it would do on the mountains of Pennsylvania. From the way he talked, he was very pleased with how it performed.

Before the Fords' visit, I think Dad was considering a newer model. After their visit, he had a whole new appreciation for his '16, so he was just going to keep it for awhile longer. A week later all that changed. Two men pulled into the lot in front of the Inn. One was driving a Model T just like the one Mr. Ford and his son drove, and he was followed by another man driving a Model T truck.

The man in the car came into the Inn and asked for Mr. McGettegen. Dad was at the desk, so he asked the man if he could help him. "Actually sir," he said, "I'm here to do something for you." He motioned Dad out onto the front porch. He then said, "You had some guests here last week, who arrived in a new '24 T."

"Yes, yes we did. It was Mr. Henry Ford and his son Edsel. They were giving one of their new cars a run to see how it would do on our mountains."

"Well, Mr. Ford enjoyed his visit with you and your family, and he asked me to give you a little something." With that, the man handed Daddy the key to a brand new 1924 Model T open touring car. Dad

looked at the man, looked at the car, turned and looked at me, and never said a word. He scratched his head, then stepped off the porch to look at *his* new car.

The gentleman explained that Mr. Ford and his son drove the car as far as Johnstown, then took the train back to Dearborn. He said they had seen enough of how it performed on the mountains.

He introduced himself as Ray Bingler, a Ford dealer in Johnstown. Mr. Ford had asked him to deliver this car personally with his thanks. "Mr. Ford also told me that I should take time to have a meal with you folks. He said he had some of the best food he ever had right here at your Inn."

The other man with Mr. Bingler was a mechanic. Bingler owned one of the largest Ford dealerships in all of Pennsylvania. He said he was proud to sell Fords, and was really pleased that Mr. Ford and his son had visited his dealership.

Mama was just getting ready to put out dinner. We had some other guests that day, and before we ate, Dad insisted on showing them his new Model T. As Dad described the car, he looked from time to time at Mr. Bingler, to see if he had anything to add. Finally Ray said, "If you wanted to sell Fords I'd hire you in a minute."

That evening we had a great meal. Mama made onion and green pepper meat loaf, peas with baby potatoes, apple sauce with raisins, a tossed salad with homemade cucumber and chive dressing, and for dessert she served Model T pie. Well, it was not Model T pie that night, but it has been Model T, or just T pie ever since. It was a banana pie, made with vanilla pudding and small pieces of pie crust running throughout the pie. It never really had a name, but that night Dad said it would be Model T pie, and to this day, that's exactly what we call it.

After dinner, Mr. Bingler and his mechanic were on their way. Even though it was getting dark, Dad insisted on going for a ride. Mama and Tinasia rode along. This was an extravagant gift, and I could tell that Dad was a bit uneasy about accepting it. He was always a better giver than he was a receiver. As we started up the mountain, we pulled in at the Graffenburg's place. Dad explained how we came to get this new car.

Having been in the lumber business most of his life, Mr. Graffenburg never had much use for a car. He always kept a big truck and a smaller truck. Dad said that since Mr. Ford was so generous with him, he wanted to give the Graffenburgs his '16 T. Mr. Graffenburg said he would like that, but insisted that he pay Daddy for it. My dad said, "That'll be just fine." You can pay me exactly as much as I paid for this one, and that's nothing."

Mr. Graffenburg still had the '16 in his barn when he died. He never got rid of it, even though he bought other cars over the years. A few years ago, a car collector came along and offered us a good bit of money for it, so we sold it to him. He said he was going to restore it. He looked at my '24 while he was here, too, but I told him I'd never part with it. We don't drive it much any more, but its just one of those things I don't want to part with. It still runs great, and from time to time I'll drive it down into McConnellsburg. And I must admit, I'm just as proud of her today as Dad and I were when we first drove it to McConnellsburg in the fall of 1924!

7

Shadow on the Moon

The years of the Great Depression meant tough economic times throughout the whole country. It started with the crash of the stock market in 1929, and it ended just about the time we got into World War II. That was in late 1941. We were fortunate at the Lincoln Inn because there were always folks who had to travel for one reason or another, and even though money was short they had to eat, and they had to have a place to sleep for the night.

During the Great Depression we gave a lot of free meals, and there were plenty of folks who stayed with us and paid only what they could. We knew we couldn't help the whole country, but we also believed that we could and should help those whose paths crossed ours.

Some folks remember the Depression years as hard times, but that is not particularly how they stand out for me. I remember other things about the Depression. As I recall, there were plenty of whole families who were moving around the country. Families from the Midwest, where everything seemed to be about the worst, came east looking for work. Because Route 30 was a main road, many of them passed right by the Lincoln Inn. I also remember how some folks who were down on their luck were still trying to make it on their own. Times were hard for them, but they were not ready to give up. They believed that better days were just ahead, and they were going to keep moving until they found them.

Mr. Franklin Roosevelt, the President, kept telling us this was true. Most folks wanted to believe him.

One particular person comes to mind when I think about the Depression years, and how folks did what they could to help each other. When I mentioned her name to Tinasia, she agreed without hesitation. This very special person was Miss Althea Michaelson Wetherby, magician, illusionist, and prestidigitator extraordinaire.

Miss Wetherby did not have a hard time during the Great Depression. She had retired shortly before we met her, and she was feeling no financial pinch. In fact, she was financially very well off, and through some "magic" she made the times a great deal easier for many folks who were not so well off. I always enjoy telling her story.

Miss Wetherby arrived at the Inn early on the afternoon of August 3, 1933. You probably wonder how I can recall the date and time so clearly. I confess I cannot recall details like that without some help. We have always kept an accurate registration book, so I looked back and found when Miss Wetherby registered.

I recall that it had rained most of that day and most of the day before. The weather was cool that early August, and there had not been much traffic by the Inn for weeks. That particular day there were only two other families staying with us. We had many such days during the Depression. For a time, Dad and I were concerned if we could keep the Inn going, but in the end we made it just fine.

When things got really slow at the Inn, Mr. Graffenburg, my father-in-law, always had some work for Dad and me, because the lumber business stayed steady during the Depression. In later years when Tinasia's father got too old to work the mill, Dad and I found odds and ends for him to do around the Inn. Tinasia and I were lucky to have families who cared for each other.

Miss Althea Michaelson Wetherby arrived at the Inn looking every bit the happiest person I had ever laid eyes on. When she walked into our main lobby, her smile lit up the room immediately. In a calm and sure voice she said, "Allow me to introduce myself, my good man. I am Miss Althea Michaelson Wetherby, magician, illusionist and prestidigitator extraordinaire! And who might you be?"

Smiling, I looked right back at her and replied, "I am Mr. Abraham Francis McGettegan, part owner, assistant manager and only-in-an-emergency cook of the Lincoln Inn, and I know for a fact I'm not extraordinary at any of them."

"And a fine Inn it is," she replied. "Do you have a room for the night?"

"Indeed we do," I replied. Turning the registration book around, I slid it across the counter to her. "Would you mind signing the registration book please?" I asked.

"Already done," she replied, clasping both hands behind her back. I turned the book around and there it was, just as clear as could be, straight as an arrow and in perfect form, "Miss Althea Michaelson Wetherby, August 3, 1933, 4:25 p.m." I couldn't believe my eyes.

"How did you do that?" I asked.

"A good magician never tells her secrets," she said flashing a warm and friendly smile. "But I suppose I could share just this one with you."

"Great," I said. "Now how did you do that?"

"Simple!" she replied. "When I came into your lobby, I quickly engaged you in conversation. If you recall, I spoke in a loud and distinct voice that caught and held your attention. You are not used to having guests sign in before you offer them the registration book, and since the book was facing you, you never even imagined that I could sign in. It also helps that I taught myself to write upside down years ago. You see, it was nothing but an illusion with a little sleight of hand, or prestidigitation, as we magicians like to call it!"

Well, whether it was magic illusion or prestidigwhatsy, I was impressed, and I knew I had made a friend. I asked if she wanted help getting her bag up to her room, or if she could do that without me noticing as well. She said no, that some help would be fine. Miss Wetherby went to her room and settled in. I took the registration book to show Mama and Tinasia. They were not real impressed because it looked like any other guest registration to them.

Even now, more than sixty years later, I have to smile when I think of Miss Wetherby. She was just the kind of person you wanted to get to know, and she was the type who would let you get to know her.

Do not ask me how or why, but I can still remember what we had for dinner that evening. Mama made wild dandelion with sweet bacon gravy, corn on the cob and fresh trout Dad and I had caught earlier in the week. Miss Wetherby particularly enjoyed the meal, and said she would favor the cook with a special illusion. That was an offer even Mama would not refuse.

Miss Wetherby asked for a length of rope and our sharpest scissors. The two youngsters who were staying with their parents in room three scrambled to get as close to her as possible. The rest of us gathered around, too. The more attention she got, the more Miss Wetherby seemed to enjoy preparing for the illusion she was about to share.

To this day, I'm not sure how she did it, but she wrapped the rope around her fingers a few times, then asked one of the children to cut it directly in half. Then she tied the two cut ends together, rubbed the piece of rope in her hands, pulled a small knot of rope off one of the ends, then produced the rope rejoined as though it had never been cut. Well, to say the least we were all impressed. We asked how she did it, but true to the magician's code of secrecy, she said with a childlike grin, "I'm not at liberty to say!"

After dinner we adjourned to the side porch. Like the rest of us, Dad was fascinated with Miss Wetherby. The evening was clear and cool, and just on the horizon, we saw a beautiful full moon rising. The rains of the past few days had finally moved out of our area. Dad said, "This is going to be a great evening to see the . . . "

Before he could finish his sentence, Miss Wetherby said, "The beautiful full moon in all its glory Mr. McGettegan!"

Dad said, somewhat puzzled, "Yes, that's right." Miss Wetherby caught his attention and winked at him. Daddy did not have a clue why she had cut him off in mid-sentence or what she was up to.

Miss Wetherby asked the two children, a boy and his little sister, if they wanted to see one of the grandest illusions in her bag of tricks. Well of course they said they did – what kid wouldn't? I was any-thing but a kid, and I wanted to see it too. They asked their parents if they could stay up to see it. Their mother hesitated, looking at their father. "Sure, that will be fine," he said.

This family was on their way from Chicago to Philadelphia. The man had lost his job as a machinist, and like so many other families, they were on their last buck. He had heard of work in Philadelphia for tool and die makers, so he sold everything they had in Chicago and moved his family east. They told Dad and me about what they were trying to do. They were not complaining about their lot in life, and they were definitely not looking for any handouts. Nonetheless it was easy to tell that the current hard times had not passed them by.

To begin her grandest illusion, Miss Wetherby pulled a small gold watch from her vest pocket, looked at it and said, "Well, we'll have to move right along." She announced that she would need a few pieces of equipment for this grand illusion. She said she needed a Mason jar filled with water, a candle, a mirror, a cork, and a penny. In short order Mama and Tinasia filled the rather unusual order.

Although she focused her attention on the children from room three, she had us all captivated. We had pulled chairs together and were sitting in a small group on the east porch. On a small table in the center of our cluster of chairs, Miss Wetherby set up a configuration of items the likes of which I had never seen before and have never seen since.

Very carefully, she set the Mason jar filled with water near the middle of the table. Directly behind the Mason jar she set the candle, which she had cut to be just exactly one half the height of the Mason jar. Just behind the candle she placed the mirror. With the same small pocket knife she used to cut the candle, she cut a small groove in the top of the cork, which she set directly in front of the Mason jar. From her pocket she produced a penny, which she inserted into the groove cut into the cork.

Again, she pulled her pocket watch out, made a mental note of the time, then explained just what she was about to do. She told us that she was about to cast a shadow on the moon. At first the children did not understand the significance of what she was about to do. They just looked at her. She repeated herself, and this time the young boy said, "You mean that candle will make that penny's shadow show on the moon?"

She said, "That's exactly what I'm about to do." Now they were both intently focused on what was about to happen. Miss Wetherby was every bit the showman. She moved from her chair to check to see if everything was positioned just correctly, then she asked the children each to check it. For effect she asked if any of the adults wanted to check it too.

She explained that the candle's light would be caught and reflected into the Mason jar by the mirror. The water in the jar would magnify the light hundreds and hundreds of times. She told us that the light coming out of the other side of the jar would be terribly bright. That light would then pass around the penny sitting on the cork and create the shadow that would be projected onto the moon. The way she explained it, I actually thought for a time that it just might happen the way she described it.

Taking one last look at her pocket watch, she asked for a match, lit the candle and told the children that since the moon moved they would see a moving shadow of the penny any time. And sure enough, a shadow began to appear on the moon. She had done such a convincing job of setting everything up, for a moment I believed that she really was casting a shadow on the moon. Then reality tapped me on the shoulder and reminded me that we were watching a lunar eclipse.

60

Just as Miss Wetherby had told them, the shadow moved across the face of the moon. They were both speechless and equally motionless. In fact, we were all kind of quiet. Fortunately, we had all caught on to what she was doing, and we did not ruin it for the kids by telling them it was an eclipse.

When the shadow finally crossed over the face of the moon, Miss Wetherby sought a reaction from the kids. They were, in a word, impressed. She asked them if they thought it was possible to cast a shadow on the moon with a candle, a mirror, a Mason jar filled with water, a cork, and a penny. The little girl, without a moment's hesitation said, "Sure it is, we just saw you do it!" Miss Wetherby did not respond, but instead looked right at the little boy. "I guess it could happen," was his reply.

Miss Althea Michaelson Wetherby had had her fun, and quickly she turned from magician to scientist. She explained to the children that the natural phenomena they had just witnessed was a lunar eclipse. She carefully explained that an eclipse happens when the earth passes between the sun and the moon. She told them that the shadow they had just seen was the shadow of the earth being projected onto the moon, not the shadow of the penny.

Then she explained the illusion she had created. She told us all, that the difference between magic and science is that in magic you do not always see what you believe to be true, and in science you do not always believe what you see. She explained that illusions are things that someone convinces you that you saw whether you did or whether you did not. At any rate the children were much impressed, and so were the adults. Miss Wetherby had made a pleasant evening for us all. The children and their parents went off to get some sleep, and so did Tinasia and Mama. My dad and I stayed up awhile and chatted with Miss Wetherby.

She told us that her father, "The Great Wetherby," had been a magician from the late 1870s until his death in 1921. Her mother, a former schoolteacher, traveled with her father as his assistant. Most of Althea's early years were spent on the road. The Wetherbys traveled from town to town, all the way from New Jersey through the Midwest and from Florida to Maine.

She told Dad and me about being fascinated with the illusions her father performed. When she was small, he actually used her from time to time, producing her from a box that did not appear much larger than a breadbox. Although her father had been successful, Althea's mother insisted that she be educated. Althea gained admission to Princeton when she was seventeen, and studied there for three years.

During her third year at Princeton, she met Thomas Alva Edison, the greatest scientist and inventor of his day. There had been a student science exhibition, and Miss Wetherby had entered a project that demonstrated how light could be bent with the use of mirrors. Mr. Edison, one of the judges at the exhibition, was much impressed with her demonstration.

Mr. Edison had a grand laboratory set up in East Orange, New Jersey, where he brought some of the brightest minds of the day. Mr. Edison's early successes with the invention of the stock ticker, the light bulb, and the phonograph made it easy for him to attract bright minds and pay them well. Miss Althea Michaelson Wetherby was one of the brightest minds he ever attracted, and he knew it right from the start.

When Miss Wetherby went to work for Mr. Edison he made her promise that she would finish college. True to her word, she did finish, and before long she was in charge of the New Jersey laboratory. Mr. Edison had opened another laboratory in Florida, and that is where he spent most of his time. Althea told Dad and me that she literally married her job. Her mother and father continued to travel, doing their magic shows until her father's death. She said her mother died shortly after her father.

At age 65, Miss Wetherby retired from the Edison laboratory, which by then was known as General Electric, a company that still is around today. She was widely regarded as one of the brightest scientists in the world. We asked her what made her decide to retire. She told Dad and me that after Mr. Edison's death in 1932, she was ready to hang it up.

We asked her why she got back into magic again after so many years. She explained that the difference between magic and science is often very slight. She also said that her early years on the road were filled with fond memories. She showed us a small picture she carried in her purse of a smiling little girl standing on top of a rather small black box. "That's me," she started, "and that's the little black box my dad used to pull me out of, until I got too big for it."

Miss Wetherby told us that she was financially very comfortable, so she could do most anything she wanted. She was very happy spending her time providing entertainment for those who were not able to afford it. She told us that most of her shows were free, and when she did raise money she generally left it to help families in the town where she performed. She said, "Life's been good to me, and I guess this is a way for me to give a little back. Besides, it's a great way for me to remember my parents."

We talked late into the night. She was truly fascinating. She told us about the last experiment she had discussed with Mr. Edison. His invention of the light bulb in 1879 revolutionized life as we know it, particularly at night. But Mr. Edison was never satisfied. He had become interested in finding a way to make a single beam of light go further without breaking up or spreading out. Years of experiments had not produced any significant results. It seemed that regardless of what they did, any beam of light they created just seemed to spread out the further it got from the source.

Althea then told us about an experiment she had tried just prior to her retirement. She said that one afternoon she had a brainstorm, while looking at a small ruby ring her father had bought her. She said she had always been fascinated with how beautiful light was when it passed through the ruby in her ring. She said she created a small beam of light and passed it through the small ruby from her ring. The beam of light projected on the wall was about the same size as the beam of light when it entered the ruby. Miss Wetherby made careful notes about what she had discovered, but she said nothing much came of it, and no one else in the lab seemed all that impressed. She laughed to herself, then said to

Dad and me, "Maybe someday someone will look at my notes and make something of them."

We ended our chat at the point where we were all exhausted. Dad and I were both humbled by the magnitude of what this magician had accomplished in her life. The next morning we chatted again over coffee and toast.

When the family from Chicago was getting ready to leave, Miss Wetherby produced coins from the children's ears and generally dazzled them again with some sleight of hand. She also had a brief, quiet conversation with their father, which ended with her handing him a small piece of paper, neatly folded in half. She left heading east for a benefit show at York Junior College.

The family from Chicago left shortly thereafter, but before they did, the man shared that Miss Wetherby had given him the name of a person to contact in Philadelphia who could find work for a good machinist. She also had neatly folded some cash into the note as well.

This next part of the story is nothing I know for sure, but I always believed it was true. You see, Dad and I have always been avid readers of the magazine *Popular Science*. There was a story in there in the late 1950s about the development of the laser beam. There was alot in the article that I could not even pretend to understand, but there was one portion of the article that I understood really well.

The laser was discovered at the laboratories of the General Electric Company, formed from what had been the old Edison Electric Company, where Miss Wetherby had worked. The article I read mentioned that laboratory notes from the 1930s had helped to launch the modern research project that led to the development of the laser. The article even mentioned lab notes that referred to the use of a simple ruby ring and a common beam of light.

There was no way I could know for sure if they were referring to the notes left by Miss Wetherby, but it suited my impression of her to believe that they were indeed her notes. And even if they were not, my impression of her was not diminished one bit. Miss Wetherby had taught us a lot during her brief visit. I knew back in 1933 she was someone I never wanted to forget. That is why I have always kept the 1863 penny she used to cast a shadow on the moon!

CHAPTER

Monopoly

The Lincoln Inn is older than computers, television, radio, stereo music players, and VCRs and DVDs. Even though we had electricity at the Inn since it was built in 1894, these new devices all came into existence since the Inn. In due time, each and every one of them has arrived at the Inn. In fact, we now have a machine hooked to the phone that can send a picture or a letter right through the phone wire. That is our FAX machine, and we have a special number so folks can send things to us.

Before we had all the things we have today to entertain us, we played lots of games. Checkers was a favorite around here. I cannot ever remember not knowing how to play checkers. Some folks played chess. Dad was really good at that. We played card games, too. My favorite was Five Hundred. I know we passed many fun hours playing that game.

We enjoyed board games, too. Sometimes our guests played them, but for the most part we played them when things were slow around the Inn. My personal favorite was Monopoly. I'm not sure just how many games we have gone through since we got our first Monopoly board, but I know it has been several.

I believe the game of Monopoly was created by Charles Darrow in 1934. Like many folks in 1934, Mr. Darrow, who lived in Germantown, Pennsylvania, was out of work. He had extra time on his hands, so he created the game of Monopoly for something to do. His game gave folks a chance, even if they were just pretending, to deal in high finances and make a fortune. The year he made his first Monopoly games he sold about 5,000 through a big Philadelphia department store. During the next year he had so many requests for games, he contacted the folks at Parker Brothers.

Since 1935, Parker Brothers has been making and selling Mr. Darrow's Monopoly game. Today, it is one of the most popular games ever created, sold in more than 30 countries, and produced in 19 foreign languages. Each year Parker Brothers prints more than $40 billion of Monopoly money, which is approximately double the amount of real money printed each year by the United States government mint in Washington.

You are probably wondering why I'm telling you all this about Monopoly. Well, the story I want to share with you centers around a Monopoly game played by two very interesting and special ladies who came to the Inn in 1991, just three years before we closed. I'm really glad they were among the last of our guests, because they proved something I believe to be true. Some folks say people do not care about each other anymore. Well, I do not believe that now; I never did believe it; and I doubt I ever will.

When they arrived at the Inn, it was a lazy afternoon in late September. The days were still plenty warm, but the nights were beginning to cool a little after a particularly hot stretch of summer during August and early September. Two couples arrived in a van sporting a bumper sticker that read, "Penn State Proud." I assumed they were from Pennsylvania, and when they registered I found out that they were.

When I happened to be standing at the desk over the years and saw folks drive up, I always played a little game. I tried first to figure out where they were from. Then I would try to guess what they did for a living. Like my dad, I have always liked talking to folks, so in short order I usually found out if I was right or not.

I guessed the two men to be brothers who owned a business together. They looked somewhat alike and a small sign painted on the door of the van read, "The Workbench Wood Emporium." I assumed they had a family business.

They did not come right into the Inn, but stood out front for a time just looking around and making small talk. One of the ladies said, "I'm sure this is the place," as she opened the front door and walked inside.

"Hello," I said.

"Hello, do you think you could find a place for the four of us tonight?"

"Sure can, that's what we're here for. And we can feed you too," I added.

"That'll be great," she said reaching for the pen beside the registration book.

"Do you want separate rooms, or would you like to share a room?"

She turned and looked at the others, and it did not look like it mattered to them one way or another. "One will be fine," she said as she wrote all of their names in the book. They were Nancy and Gerald Glenn, and Christy and Michael Milton. I asked what line of work they were in and found that both of the Glenns were teachers from Ligonier, Pennsylvania. Mr. Milton was a freelance writer who operated a small specialty woodworking shop and country emporium near Bedford, Pennsylvania. Mrs. Milton was also a teacher. When I found out that they were from Bedford, I asked if they knew Gracie and Buck. Mr. Milton said he had heard of Dr. Buckman, but did not know him personally.

Nancy and Christy had walked away from the desk and were checking out the place. Tinasia came out of the kitchen and immediately recognized Christy. "Well, you did indeed make it back."

"Yes we did, and our friends are with us," Christy said. Later, Tinasia told me that Mrs. Milton and her husband had been through that past May. She said they were driving by, thought the Lincoln Inn looked like a charming place, and stopped to inquire about rooms and meals. She had told Tinasia at the time that they always planned a getaway weekend with another couple each year in late September. Mrs. Milton said they looked to find a place each year that would be quiet and relaxing without alot of distractions.

After they registered, we took their bags to their room. In short order, they left to scout out a good fishing spot for the men for the following morning. It was nearly 2:00 p.m. We had guests in two of the other rooms, and Tinasia had planned supper for 5:30. Mr. Glenn said, "That'll be fine. We've just got to find a spot to take a few worms swimming in the morning. If we're running late, don't hold dinner up just on our account."

Mr. Milton asked what we would be having. Tinasia said she was fixing meat loaf with onion and green pepper gravy, home-made buttermilk biscuits, fresh green beans almondine from our garden, boiled turnips in bacon sauce and banana splits for desert. "On second thought," Mr. Milton said, "we'll be back early for a meal like that!"

They were back early, and while we waited for Tinasia to get things ready, Jerry, Mike, and I chatted on the side porch. They had found a perfect spot to fish near Caledonia State Park, just on the other side of Chambersburg. Mike talked about his business and told Jerry he needed to stay busy now that he was retired. I had assumed they were all in their early to mid-fifties, and when he said they were all around retirement age I knew I was right. Both of their wives were still teaching, with plans to retire at the end of the current school year.

I wondered how they had met. As if they had read my mind, they said their wives had met a few years ago about this time. They were both in the same hospital scheduled for the same surgery on the same day. They were nearly the same age and they were both teachers. "Well, with that much in common," Mike said, "they became imme-diate friends. Besides, with what they were facing the next day, they had a common bond."

The men grew quiet. Jerry broke the awkward silence by saying, "And that's when Mike and I met."

Tinasia called us to supper and as usual it was great. As best I can recall, I only ever had three bad meals at the Lincoln Inn. The night Gracie was born Daddy made dinner, and even at my tender age, I knew cooking was not his strong point. Once when Tinasia and Mama stayed over with Gracie and Buck in Bedford,

I tried to cook for Dad and me. I guess I paid him back and showed him that cooking was not my strong suit, either. The third bad meal was the one and only time Mom and Tinasia got the bright idea to fix liver and onions.

After dinner folks sat around and chatted for awhile. Tinasia served coffee. We had recently bought a big screen TV with a stereo VCR. It came with a couple of movies and we had bought a good many more. I'm not much on TV and never really have been, but the guests seem to enjoy it, so we have had TV at the Inn since shortly after World War II. That night I believe we watched the movie *Hopscotch*.

Before going up to their room, Mrs. Glenn and Mrs. Milton asked if we had a Monopoly game. Tinasia said she knew right where it was and she started to get it. "No, please don't bother now, we'd just like to use it tomorrow if we could." Tinasia said she would get it out and leave it on the desk after breakfast.

The next morning, the guests who were checking out had breakfast and were on their way early. Jerry and Mike also were up early and on their way. They were surprised that Tinasia and I were already up and that Tinasia had fixed them an ample bag lunch that would cover breakfast and lunch. She told them that dinner would be served at 5:30, but that if the fish were biting she would warm something up for them whenever they got back. As I've said over and over, the Lincoln Inn has always been a place where folks were treated right.

True to her word and her good memory, Tinasia had no trouble finding the Monopoly board. It was an older game that had been used often in some long and hard games. Several billion dollars probably changed hands over that board. When Mrs. Nancy Glenn and Mrs. Christy Milton came downstairs, the first thing they asked for was the Monopoly game. I motioned toward a small table I had set up along the east wall of the dining room. I thought they could play there and take advantage of the morning sun. Even though it was only September, there was an early morning coolness in the air and the warmth of the sun coming through the tall windows that looked out onto the side porch felt really good.

Tinasia set the ladies up at the big table. As I recall, they both just asked for toast and coffee. They engaged in some small talk. I was curious to know if they planned on playing Monopoly all day, or if they had plans while the husbands fished. I did not want to come right out and ask, but since I was somewhat fond of the game myself, I was interested in just how long they thought it might take to play a game.

Everyone approaches the game of Monopoly a bit differently. To some folks it is just a casual game with little meaning or consequence. To others it is a match of wits, brains, and the power to bargain. I suppose I have always taken the game seriously, and although I have been bested a time or two, I will admit I see the game as a real challenge and a personal test every time I put my car on the board. Oh yes, I'm always the car – never, ever have I played with any other marker on the board.

The ladies did not respond directly to my question. Mrs. Milton looked at Mrs. Glenn, shrugged her shoulders and said, "If it's like most games, we'll be here most of the morning and a good part of the afternoon." Then she turned to me and said, "Is that a problem?"

"No, not at all! You can play as long and hard as you like, but I must warn you we don't tolerate any fist fighting around the Inn," I joked.

Mrs. Glenn teased back, "Well, we really get into a good game of Monopoly, but we haven't taken to beating each other up yet. We'll keep your rule about fist fighting in mind."

After they finished, Tinasia cleared the table, and the ladies moved to the little table I had set up for them. They noticed the warmth of the sun and commented how good it felt. In no time they had the board set up and they were into it full swing. It was a little after 10:00 a.m.

I was not doing much that day other than fixing a few odds and ends around the Inn. From time to time, I passed the ladies as they played. They were sharing some light conversation, but for the most part they were focused on their game. On one trip through the Inn, I heard Christy say to Nancy, "I'll give you my North Carolina for your New York." Looking right at her friend she expected an immediate answer that did not come.

"No!" Nancy replied. "That would give you a monopoly and I'd still need Pacific Avenue for a monopoly."

"Ok, how 'bout if I throw in, say $200.00?"

Nancy's reply did not change. "No, I still won't have a monopoly, so how will I get any money? And besides, you always go for those orange properties every year."

The phrase "every year" caught my attention. It almost sounded like they got together each year just for a game of Monopoly. My curiosity was piqued, but I did not dare ask, because after all it was really none of my business.

Tinasia served a rather simple lunch of fresh fruit, cottage cheese, small cubes of cheese and cold meat, and freshly-baked rye bread. There were only four of us having lunch, since no other guests had checked in. I asked about their progress, and each of the ladies chidingly blamed the other for the slow progress of the game. At one point Nancy looked down at her plate and said, "But then again, we're in no hurry. There was a dramatic change in the tone and temper of her voice that Christy picked up on immediately. I sensed a real show of emotion, but I had no clue what caused it.

"Hey, this is great," Christy said, quickly changing the mood back to where it had been.

"Yes it is," Nancy said. "This is a great place too."

We finished lunch, and talked about a variety of things from gardening to retirement. Nancy asked if Tinasia and I ever thought of retiring. We looked at each other, pondered the question for a bit, then Tinasia said, "I suppose we've thought about it, but we've never really done anything about it. Mac says he's going to retire when he turns 100, so I guess I'll retire with him then."

"When will you be 100, Mac?" Christy asked me.

"In three years, on April 18, 1994, and that night, I'm closing the place, once and for all." I shared the story about how the Inn opened the day I was born, and the ladies agreed my 100th birthday was an excellent time to close her down for good. They both said they could not believe that Tinasia and I were in our mid-90s. I have always liked it when people say that. I suppose it makes me feel younger than I really am.

After lunch the ladies went out onto the side porch for a time, but then they were quickly back to their game. Tinasia got busy with supper, and I continued my "putzing around. "Putzing around" is a phrase my dad always used to describe doing little things that were not very important or difficult, but necessary just the same.

Their game continued well into the afternoon. On another of my trips through the lobby, I heard them dealing for Connecticut Avenue and Ventnor Avenue. Mentally, I tried to match colors with these avenues. I remembered that Connecticut was pale blue, but it took me a little while to recall that Ventnor was bright yellow. I guess it had been too long since I had played a game myself. This deal did not go any better than the first one I had overheard. I glanced at the board and saw only a few houses and even fewer hotels.

They had been at it for nearly five hours, and neither one was anywhere close to winning. They each had their deeds laid out along their side of the table, and their money was neatly stacked beside the deeds they had accumulated over the past five hours. There was a relaxed sense about this game, but at the same time, you got the notion that there was a sense of purpose to it.

By 4:30 in the afternoon, the game was over. I came through the lobby to get a cup of coffee and settle down with the evening paper that had just been dropped off. I noticed that the board and all of its pieces were neatly back in the box, the closed box was in the middle of the small table, and the ladies had gone to their room. Tinasia was busy in the kitchen, and she had not heard them leave.

Mr. Milton and Mr. Glenn were back well before 5:00. They reported that it had been a good day, "but throwing them back seemed better than keeping them today," Mr. Milton said. A minister from Chicago on his way to Philadelphia had checked in about 3:00, and a couple from Denver, Colorado, on their way to Boston for a grandson's wedding checked in just after 5:00.

As always, we had a great dinner. Everyone seemed to get along well and engaged in good conversation. I've always enjoyed that. In fact, I've never been much for eating alone. Dad always said good conversation improves a good meal and makes the food digest better. I believe he was right about that.

Just after dinner the Glenns and the Miltons checked out. Both Nancy and Christy thanked us for our hospitality and said how much they enjoyed their visit to the Inn. I asked who had won the Monopoly game. They just looked at each other and said, "We're never really sure who wins, maybe we'll figure that out next year."

There was that yearly comment again. Now I was sure of it. These two ladies came together each year for a Monopoly game. Not that it was any concern of mine, but I wondered why two ladies would travel to our Inn that was not really close to either of their homes to play a game of Monopoly for no apparent reason.

Before they left, Mrs. Milton handed me a thick brown envelope addressed to the Pennsylvania State University Hospital, Milton S.

Hershey Medical Center, Hershey, Pennsylvania. She asked me to mail it in the morning, since they did not know where the nearest mailbox was located. I noticed that it did not have a return address, and when I asked her she said, "We may be moving soon, would you mind using the return address of the Inn?" That was fine with me.

The next morning, I gave the thick brown envelope to the mailman and he assured me that it would be on its way later that afternoon. I was curious about what was in the envelope, but I assumed I would never know.

The following Thursday morning Tinasia came out onto the side porch to let me know that I had a phone call. She looked kind of puzzled when she said it was a doctor calling from the Hershey Medical Center. Immediately, I thought of Nancy, Christy, and the brown envelope they had given me. I went inside to take the call.

The doctor asked if I was Mr. McGettegan, and I said I was. He asked if we had recently had two guests at the Inn named Nancy Glenn and Christy Milton. I told him that they had been with us the previous week and their husbands were with them. I asked him if his call had anything to do with the brown envelope. I tried to tell him that I knew nothing about the envelope. The doctor laughed and said, "I know you have no idea what was in there, and I'll bet she told you that she was moving to get you to use your return address." I told him he was right on target.

My curiosity was about to explode when he offered to explain. He said that seven years ago, Mrs. Milton and Mrs. Glenn met at the Medical Center in Hershey the evening before they were both to have surgery. After visiting hours, both ladies were more than a little anxious about what the next day would bring. Both faced a similar surgery that was life-threatening. Immediately, there was a bond between them.

To pass the time that long evening, a nurse offered a number of board games, cards, or video tapes. Nancy and Christy chose Monopoly. Each of them had played and enjoyed the game numerous times as they had raised their families. Nancy was the mother of five and Christy had two children.

Well, the next day, both of the ladies went through surgery with little difficulty. The doctor explained that he had operated on both of them, one right after the other. He said both faced treatments after the surgery and the long-term prognosis for each of them was positive. They had faced a similar challenge and together mustered what it took to meet it and beat it.

One year after their initial surgery the ladies met again. By coincidence, they were staying at the same hotel in Hershey the night before they were scheduled for an annual checkup. The doctor told me that every year since then, they have made it a point to spend some time together in September. He said, "This year they chose your Inn for this annual reunion."

I asked him, "Do you mean they just get together to play Monopoly and give their husbands a chance to fish?"

"On the surface it may look that way, but there's a little more to it. Actually, there is a lot more to it." He paused for a minute then continued. He asked if I had a Monopoly board handy and I told him I did. He asked me to get it, pull out the instruction sheet, and turn to the directions on how much money each player receives at the beginning of the game. Tinasia was standing with me as I did what the doctor suggested. I had to admit that I had no idea what I was doing or why I was doing it.

"Do you have the instructions?" he asked as I picked up the phone again. I said I did. He then said, "Ok, now read the part about dividing up the initial money."

I turned to that part and read, "Each player is given $1500 divided as follows: two each of $500s, $100s and $50s; 6 - $20s; five each of $10s, $5s and $1s."

"Mr. McGettegan, how much money would then be distributed to start a game between two people?" the doctor on the other end of the phone asked.

"Why $3,000 I suppose."

"Well, the thick brown envelope you mailed for Nancy and Christy contained 30 real $100 bills. Each and every year they have made a similar contribution to be used here at the Medical Center for folks going through what they did."

"You see," he continued, "this is their way of remembering a tough time they shared and the comfort they gained from each other's company and a simple Monopoly game."

I was totally dumbfounded. I explained to the doctor that I had picked up on the fact that their game was somewhat of an annual thing, but that was all I knew. He went on to tell me that I would more than likely be hearing from them soon. He thanked me for the little part Tinasia and I, and the Lincoln Inn had played. He said the ladies always send cash and they like their gift to be as anonymous as possible. He said they always use the return address of where they stay for their visit so their "gift" is not accidentally lost in the mail.

Sure enough, we did hear from the ladies that next week. A small package arrived in the mail. In it were two Monopoly coffee mugs and a small note that read, "Thanks for your help!" The note was signed "Christy and Nancy."

9

Mr. President

As I've mentioned before, the design of the Lincoln Inn was rather simple. The Inn has two stories. The eleven guest rooms are on the second floor. There are six bathrooms, with two rooms sharing each of five baths. Room number one has its own private bath. My mother called room one the "Presidential Suite." She did so for good reason. Let me explain.

Over the years that we have lived here on the mountain, the Graffenburg family and my family have purchased most of the land around the Inn. Today, most of what we do not own is owned by the state. As a youngster I always had free run of the whole mountainside, and I enjoyed it. Quite honestly, I doubt if there is a single square foot of this mountain that I have not touched at one time or another.

My dad and Mr. Graffenburg always hunted, and as soon as I was old enough I started hunting too. We enjoyed small game hunting mostly, but now and again we would take a deer or two as well. Mama and Tinasia never cared much for the wild meat, as they called it, but they were good about fixing it for us. Often, we had enough to share with the guests. Mr. Graffenburg and Daddy were particularly fond of squirrel.

As I recall, I was about twelve years old when I really got interested in hunting. Most days after school I rushed home, changed clothes, and was off to the woods until supper. Saturdays, I finished my chores early, then I was off to the woods. Sometimes I went by myself and other times, with my dad or Mr. Graffenburg.

One particular Saturday, October 8, 1906, I was in the woods by myself. I carried a brand new .22 that my parents had bought me for my birthday that year. I was squirrel hunting. If you have never hunted for squirrel, you may not know that you have to sit very quiet. Squirrels can hear and see real well, and they can detect the slightest movement.

We followed two simple rules about hunting on the mountain. Above all, we emphasized safety. We knew that guns were dangerous, so we were careful with them. And, we practiced good sportsmanship. Daddy said it was not right to be any other way about hunting and fishing.

On this particular Saturday in 1906, I was sitting at the base of a tree as quietly as I could, when I heard some men coming down the mountain behind me. They certainly were not being quiet. They were laughing and talking as they walked among the trees. They spotted me and one of the men shouted, "Hello young fellow, having any luck today?" He had a broad smile and a booming voice that carried as though he was standing right next to me.

"Nothing yet," I answered.

As they came closer, I thought I recognized the man who had hollered to me. "No way, I told myself. It can't be. Why would he be hunting on my mountain? But the closer he got, the more he looked like who I thought he was. He was not hunting because he carried no gun. In an instant he removed all doubt.

Hello, young man. I'm Teddy, and who are you?"

'I'm. . . , I'm a. . . , I'm Mac McGettegen."

"Well, Mac McGettegen, it's a pleasure to meet you."

"These are my friends, Colonel Jeffards and Mr. Vallandingham."

Ignoring the other two gentlemen, I said, "You're President Roosevelt."

"Yes I am, but my friends just call me Teddy, and if you want to be friends, you can call me Teddy too. Do you live around here, Mac?" Mr. Roosevelt asked.

"Yes, my parents run the Lincoln Inn out along the main road."

"Sure, I remember passing it on our way in. What time do they serve lunch," he asked?

"Usually about noon. I was going to start down soon, I'll gladly take you to the Inn."

"That would be fine, Mac."

As we started down the mountain, President Roosevelt explained to me why he was making a visit to a remote piece of forest land in Pennsylvania. Congress was planning to turn over some federal lands to the state. He said he was very interested in conservation, and wanted to make sure that there would always be plenty of natural areas throughout the country. Some of the land on the other side of our mountain had once been federal land and now it was going to become Pennsylvania state lands. Today, it is still Pennsylvania state game land.

When we reached the Inn, I tried to figure out how to introduce the President of the United States and his two friends to my parents. Over the years, I had brought alot of things back from my trips into the woods, but how many twelve-year-olds go hunting and come home having bagged the President of the United States?

As we approached the Inn, I saw Mama walk onto the side porch to ring the large hand bell she used to call me when Daddy was not around to whistle. Just as she started to ring the bell, we stepped around the corner. Before I could say a word, Mr. Roosevelt took off his floppy, broad-brimmed hat and said, "Good afternoon Mrs. McGettegen, are we in time for lunch?"

My mother just smiled and said, "Yes, indeed you are! I was just about to serve. We don't have any guests today, so it will just be some warmed-over potato soup and cold ham sandwiches.

"Sounds marvelous. These are my friends Gunther and Alonzo," Mr. Roosevelt said pointing respectively to Colonel Jefferds and Mr. Vallandingham.

"It's a pleasure to meet you, gentlemen. Come on in and get warm. I just started a fire. Mac, check your gun and put it in the cellar."

It had been a chilly morning and the heat from the fire felt good. Mama moved a small table near the fireplace and that is where Mr. Roosevelt and his friends were sitting when I came into the dining room. Mama was explaining that Daddy had gone to McConnellsburg to pick up a load of groceries, and that he would be back soon. As I came through the kitchen, Mama spotted me and said, "Mac come in here and get warm by the fire."

I do not know what I expected, but Mama was just treating them like any other guests. She had to know that he was the President of the United States. He had introduced himself, so even if she had not recognized him, there was no excuse. I think I expected her to get out the good china, and set the big table and make something special. After all, he was "The President," and these were his two friends.

Instead, Mama served just what she had offered--warmed-over potato soup and cold ham sandwiches. Mr. Roosevelt had kicked off his boots, and was warming his feet by the fire. The gentlemen had taken off their coats and hung them over the backs of their chairs. If I had not known any better, I would have assumed that they were just three regular guys who happened in from the forest, looking for something simple to eat and a place to get warm.

Colonel Jefferds and Mr. Vallandingham did not say much, but Mr. Roosevelt talked freely. He complimented Mama over and over on the soup and the sandwiches. His appetite was as big as his smile and his voice, and I will never forget how he talked to me like we were old friends. He asked me to tell him about the mountain and I did. I was proud of our mountain because it was ours.

Grace often slept in on Saturday mornings, and lunch became breakfast for her. When she came out this particular morning, she paid little attention to the four of us eating near the fireplace. She went straight into the kitchen. Mama brought her out and introduced her to our special guests. Mr. Roosevelt greeted her with a broad smile and said, "You look just like my Alice Lee did when she was a little girl. It's nice to meet you. My friends call me Teddy. What's your name?"

"Well, my real name is Grace, but everybody calls me Gracie."

Mr. Roosevelt put his arms out and offered Grace a seat on his lap. He said, "Well I'd like to be your friend, so I think I'll just call you Gracie, if that's okay with you."

"Sure, we can be friends," Gracie said as she crawled up on his lap. She acted like she knew him all her life. I still kept thinking we should be treating him special or something.

Mama brought Grace a bowl of oatmeal. Her hair was mussed from sleeping, and she was still in her pajamas. She wore Dr. Dentons that had the feet in them, like slippers. Mr. Roosevelt kept talking to us, and Grace paid him little attention. She sat on the lap of the President of the United States just the same as if she were sitting on one of our dining room chairs.

When Daddy got back from McConnellsburg he was, to say the least, shocked when he walked into the Inn. He read the paper daily and he recognized Mr. Roosevelt and both of his friends. Daddy even knew why they were here. He and our guests hit it off immediately. Mama set a place at the table for him. After everyone else was served Mama joined us, sitting at the corner of the main dining table. She wanted to stay close to the kitchen in case anyone needed something.

Like he did with all of our guests, Daddy and Mr. Roosevelt chatted about a number of things. One of our guests, a salesman who came through on a regular basis, once told my dad that he liked staying with us because the Inn had a comfortable, homey feeling. He said he particularly liked the way my dad could talk to anyone. Daddy thanked him and said, "Any guest of ours gets the same treatment, even if he happens to be the President of these United States." Well, true to his word, Daddy treated Mr. Roosevelt just as he did any other guest — warm and friendly.

When I was done, I carried my bowl and plate into the kitchen, then came back and curled up on one of the big chairs along the sides of the dining room. Mr. Roosevelt was busy explaining how the government was going to turn federal lands over to the states. He asked Mr. Vallandingham, who was one of his aides, to explain the details of the program. All that made sense to me was that it was land that no one could ever build on. As I recall, Daddy agreed with him.

They talked on into the afternoon. Mama kept them supplied with coffee. Gracie and I set up a checkerboard on a corner of the dining room table to entertain ourselves. The conversation about conservation, reforestation and the importance of undeveloped watersheds was a bit much for us.

Late in the afternoon Mr. Roosevelt asked if Dad could drive him down the mountain toward McConnellsburg. He and his friends had driven up from Washington, and had left their car along the road just above McConnellsburg. While they were gone, Mama sent Gracie and me off to get cleaned up for dinner. She had laid out our Sunday School clothes. She said she had invited the Graffensburgs down for dinner too.

When Dad, Mr. Roosevelt, and his friends arrived back at the Inn, Mr. Roosevelt asked if we could give them a room for the night. Daddy said he was happy they were staying, and Mama told them that supper would be ready about 5:30. She also said she had invited some neighbors. Mr. Roosevelt asked what we would be having and Mama said, "We'll have pan-fried, lean-cut pork chops, buttered lima beans, honey and brown sugar glazed carrots, boiled new potatoes and warm whole-wheat bread. And for dessert, I have some apple cinnamon cake and vanilla ice cream.

"Sounds great to me Mrs. McGettegen, we're staying."

"Please call me Arlene," Mama said.

"Well, I'd like to, but then you have to stop calling me Mr. Roosevelt. I'll call you Arlene, but you have to call me Teddy."

Mama just smiled and said, "Okay, Teddy, that's fine with me."

Daddy showed the men to their rooms. He put Mr. Roosevelt in room number one, the big room at the top of the stairs, with a view of Route 30. It was the biggest of all the guest rooms, and it was the only one that had its own bathroom. Colonel Jeffards and Mr. Vallandingham stayed in room number two, right next to Mr. Roosevelt's room.

Vallandingham, an older fellow with snow white hair, was a long-time friend of Mr. Roosevelt, and served as one of his aides. Their close friendship had been formed during the time when Mr. Roosevelt was a cowboy. Even though he had been raised New York City, Mr. Roosevelt always liked the West. When his wife and his mother both died on the same day, he decided to spend some time there. He stayed there for a few years before coming back and going into politics. When he came back to New York, he married for a second time.

Colonel Jeffards was much younger. He was a big man, and just from looking at him you got the idea he was very strong. Later, Daddy told me he was a guard for Mr. Roosevelt. Today, they call presidential guards the Secret Service. Jeffards and Roosevelt got to know each other when Mr. Roosevelt was the governor of New York. At first they were just friends, but then Mr. Jeffards became a guard at the governor's mansion. When Mr. Roosevelt became president, he personally selected Gunther Jeffards to be his personal guard. I had the idea that these three men were good friends.

Grace and I got ready for dinner early, so we were the first two in the dining room. We played checkers again, just to pass the time. Mr. Roosevelt came down the steps into the dining room, dressed in a tweed suit with knickers and mid-length leather riding boots. He joined Gracie and me for a round of checkers, while we waited for everyone else to come to the table. He played each of us a game, and Gracie and I both won. It was nice of him to let us win. How many kids could ever say they beat the President of the United States at checkers?

When the Graffenburgs arrived, they had the same reaction I did. They knew Mr. Roosevelt was there, but they seemed shocked to see him just the same. Tinasia came with them, and was dressed in her Sunday School clothes too. When Mr. Roosevelt was introduced to her, he shook her hand, then kissed her on the head. It was obvious to me that he really liked kids. During the evening he told us about his children. I cannot remember all their names, but I think he had five children. He told us that they really liked animals, and they kept many at the White House. His children even had a pony, that they rode in the big ballroom at the White House. Their pony had rubber shoes that would not mark the floor in the White House.

After everyone gathered in the dining room, Mama invited us to sit down. Daddy offered Mr. Roosevelt the seat at the head of the table, but he quickly pulled out one of the chairs along the side. As he did he said, "Thank you Francis, but this is your home, and your table. I'm your guest and happy to be here, but you are the head of this house and that's your seat. And thank you for being so gracious."

Mama served the evening meal, and like always it was great. Mr. Roosevelt and his friends really appreciated it, and they complimented Mama several times. When the meal was over, we all sat around and talked for quite awhile. Mr. Roosevelt told lots of stories and each one was more interesting than the one before. He told about being in Africa and hunting big game, and he told about the time when he was a cowboy out west. He had a way of telling stories that really held our attention.

I can remember bits and pieces of a number of the stories Mr. Roosevelt told, but one sticks out in my mind clearer than any other. It was a story about a certain bear that he encountered during one of his hunting trips.

Mr. Roosevelt said he was hunting bear in one of the southern states. I believe it was Kentucky. One particular day, they had hunted most of the morning with no luck. After they took a break for lunch, their guide suggested they go to an entirely different part of the forest. Mr. Roosevelt said he later learned that another guide who had gotten up early that morning had trapped a small bear. He tied the bear to a tree, then came back to the camp. That was why their guide had directed them to that section of the forest for the afternoon.

As the hunting party made its way through the woods, they came across the bear. The guide quickly ran ahead. He told Mr. Roosevelt to come to the clearing where the bear had been tied and he would let it go. He said Mr. Roosevelt could shoot it and have a fine trophy from his hunting trip.

Mr. Roosevelt said he appreciated the time the guide had taken, but he refused to shoot a bear that had been trapped and tied to a tree. He told the guide that he liked to hunt big game, but that he did it for the sport, not just to kill something. He told the guide to untie the bear and let it go. The guide did as he was told.

News of this story spread fast. Even though Mr. Roosevelt was known as a big game hunter, he quickly earned a reputation for being a humane sportsman and a president who was interested in the conservation of wildlife, forest lands, and other natural resources. To this day, no president has done more to protect the environment than Theodore Roosevelt.

He went on to tell us that later that same year, a toy manufacturer from New York had an idea for a toy bear, inspired by the bear he refused to shoot. The man's name was Morris Michtom and he made toys and candy in New York City. Mr. Michtom called him at the White House, to ask his permission to make a bear like the one Mr. Roosevelt refused to shoot. Mr. Roosevelt said he didn't see anything wrong with making a toy bear, but he also didn't know what Mr. Michtom planned to do with the bears once he made them.

Mr. Roosevelt had so many stories to tell that he interrupted himself from time to time. As the evening went on Mama kept everyone supplied with coffee. For us kids, she made hot chocolate. I pretended it was coffee, so I would be like one of the adults.

When Mr. Roosevelt finished one cup of coffee he said, "That was good to the last drop," then laughed. He explained that during a visit to the Maxwell House Hotel in New York City two years ago, he made that comment about a cup of coffee that was specially made for the Maxwell House Hotel. Someone had picked up on his comment, and figured that since the President of the United States said the coffee was "good to the last drop," it had to be true. Soon the coffee was being sold as Maxwell House coffee. Even today, more than 90 years later, the Maxwell House coffee slogan is still "good to the last drop!"

After the coffee story, Mr. Roosevelt went back to his story about the toy bears Mr. Michtom made. He said the first bears were small, plush, doll-like toys with black eyes and noses, and a red ribbon around the neck. Mr. Michtom sent him one of the first bears he made shortly before last Christmas. As with most things a president does, it made the newspapers all over the country. The picture that was carried with the newspaper stories featured President Theodore Roosevelt sitting at his desk in the White House with a small, plush, toy bear sitting on his desk. Mr. Roosevelt was smiling in the picture.

The stories that accompanied the picture varied quite a bit. Many of the articles embellished the story to make it more interesting. According to Mr. Roosevelt, though, the simple truth was that he loved to hunt, but he was a sportsman, and no true sportsman would shoot a trapped animal. He did not mind that the story got a lot of play in the papers, because it helped to make people aware of hunting as a sport, and the need for natural resource and wildlife management.

Gracie was growing tired, and she must have known that Mr. Roosevelt was not quite finished with his story. She walked over to his chair, crawled up on his lap, and hugged him. Then she said, "Thanks. I'm glad you didn't shoot the bear." Everyone in the room chuckled.

"Well Gracie, I'm glad too," Mr. Roosevelt said. "Jeffards, she looks like your little Molly sitting here."

"I have a daughter named Molly, and she and Mr. Roosevelt have become good friends," Mr. Jeffards said.

"I love kids; I never have met one I couldn't be friends with," the President said. In a few minutes, Gracie was sound asleep on Mr. Roosevelt's lap.

The President told us that the bears were going to be sold again this year around Christmas. He told us that just the week before, he had walked over to the Treasury Department building in Washington, and on the way he was greeted by a window full of Mr. Michtom's bears. He said they were right in the main window of F. A. O. Schwarz's Toy store, at the corner of J and 10th Streets. A small sign above the bears read, "Teddy Bears--Just Arrived From New York City." As part of his window display, Mr. Schwarz had a picture of Mr. Roosevelt sitting at his desk, holding his "Teddy" bear.

Mr. Roosevelt told us he was flattered. He said, "I hope these little brown Teddies make a lot of kids happy." He went on to say, "And I suppose if I'm not remembered for anything else, being remembered as a plush and cuddly friend to a lot of kids will do just fine."

Shortly after Mr. Roosevelt finished his story, Mama said it was time for Gracie and me to go to bed. I looked at the clock and it was after 2:00 a.m. Tinasia had fallen asleep on her dad's lap so the Graffenburgs decided to stay the night in one of the guest rooms.

The next morning we were all up early for breakfast. Mr. Roosevelt, Colonel Jeffards, and Mr. Vallandingham were anxious to get back to Washington. Mr. Roosevelt made a few calls from the phone in the lobby while Mama set breakfast on the table.

As the President and his party left, Mr. Roosevelt thanked Mama and Dad over and over. It was obvious that he was very appreciative. Then he said something that has always stuck with me. I kept thinking that we should have treated him special because of who he was. He thanked us for just the opposite. I can even remember what he said. "Thanks for a great day, and especially thanks for treating us just like you would any other guests. You gave us a chance to relax and just be ourselves, and that's always appreciated."

About a week after this memorable visit, we got the nicest letter from Mr. Roosevelt. Enclosed with the letter was his photograph, with a note handwritten across the bottom. It read, "Thanks to all my friends at the Lincoln Inn, Teddy." Of course, we had the picture framed and it still hangs in the room Mama named the Presidential Suite.

Gracie and I liked seeing the picture, but it was not until we got older that we appreciated it. Mr. Roosevelt sent us something that was far more to our liking just before Christmas of that year. He sent each of us a "Teddy Bear" from that toy store in Washington, DC.

I suppose the Teddy Bears made over the years would number in the billions. The joy, happiness, and comfort Mr. Michtom's bears have brought to children everywhere can never be measured and I for one believe they could not be named after a better president. The man for whom the Teddy Bear is named was one of the kindest, gentlest, and friendliest guests ever to stay at the Lincoln Inn.

10

The Band

Numerous times over the past 100 years, the Lincoln Inn has had a chance to extend a little generosity to someone in need. Dad always said, "Help someone in need and the experience will do you both some good!" I think he was right. I can recall a number of folks we have helped, but I cannot recall them all. I am glad I can't because if I could, that would mean we did not take the time to help enough.

One family that comes to mind told us there was no way they could pay us, but they needed a meal and a place to sleep for the night. That was not a problem. As I remember, they did not even have enough money to get where they were headed. They blew a tire just up the mountain from the Inn, and they had no money to have it fixed. The man had lost his small farm in Illinois when the bank forclosed on it. The man had a brother in Connecticut, and he was headed there with his family hoping to find some work. Dad gave them a used tire to get them back on the road, and I gave them a little money. Tinasia and Mama gave them food to take along.

The man's wife gave Mama a hug when they left and said she would repay her some day. Mama said, "Never mind repaying us. When you're on your feet again, help someone else and tell them to pass it on." My folks taught me early on that help is not something that needs to be repaid.

When we helped folks, we never expected anything in return, but there was a time when the hospitality of the Lincoln Inn was repaid in grand style. The repayment was unlike anything that had ever happened at the Inn before or since. I can recall the incident as clearly as though it happened just yesterday.

It was the late spring of 1951, and everything around the Inn had come into bloom early. That spring had been particularly warm, so by late May the setting around the Inn looked like early summer. I was out on the lawn on the east side of the Inn when a large silver bus pulled into the lot. It was too long to fit into a regular parking spot, so the driver edged the bus up close to the side of the Inn. There was smoke coming from around the wheels in the back of the bus and a strong odor of something that was burning or was very hot.

"Where's the nearest garage?" the driver yelled out to me, trying to be heard above the sound of the bus.

"McConnellsburg, about six miles in that direction," I said, pointing west and gesturing up over the mountain.

"I think my brakes are about gone," the driver said.

"Well, you don't want to try and go to McConnellsburg with bad brakes. It's a long downhill run and it can be tricky even with good brakes. Shut it down and let's take a look. There are some fellows here who are pretty good with cars and small trucks, and maybe they'll know what to do." I was referring to Dad and my father-in-law, Mr. Graffenburg. They were as good as any two guys I knew when it came to tinkering with machines. Between them there was not much they could not do.

Just then the door of the bus opened. A stately-looking gentleman stepped off the bus. He was dressed in a long swallow-tailed black coat, over grey pinstriped trousers, with a white shirt topped by a stiffly starched collar, a handsome black bow tie and white spats over his polished black shoes. His silver hair was smartly parted in the middle and his silver mustache was neatly curled at either end. His pince-nez glasses were clipped tightly to the bridge of his nose.

"I am Maestro Alfred Longwood McCambridge," the man said in a quiet and polite voice. "I am the conductor of the symphony orchestra and choir of the University of Pittsburgh. We seem to be having a bit of a problem. Can you help us?"

"I'm Mac McGettegen, and I'm pleased to meet you," I said extending my hand to shake his.

In a formal tone, he said, "We seem to be having a bit of trouble with our bus. Would you be so good as to give us directions to the nearest garage?"

"Well, like I told your driver, the nearest garage is on the other side of that mountain," I said pointing west again, "and I don't think it's wise to risk it with brake problems."

"Hummm, we do have a bit of trouble don't we," the Maestro continued.

"I'd say you do, but let's see if my dad and my father-in-law have any ideas."

"Are they mechanics? the Maestro asked

"Well, there isn't much they can't fix when they put their minds to it." The conductor just stood there looking puzzled. I don't think he liked my answer so I clarified it just a bit. "You see sir, we're kind of out in the country here, and a man's got to learn how to fix most things he has to work with. So no, they aren't mechanics in the strictest sense of the word, but if given time, I'll bet they will be able to help you out. And besides, six miles of downhill road stretch between your bus with bad brakes and the nearest mechanic."

"I see. Well, shall we call them and see what they can do?"

"Sure, let me just step inside and given them a ring. My dad is up at my inlaws' house helping with something."

My mother came out onto the side porch and asked what was going on. I gave her a quick explanation, and just then the other bus pulled in. The symphony orchestra was on one bus and the choir was on the other. The drivers chatted and for a time they thought of trying to load the students all on one bus, but I discouraged that idea. These folks had come down from Pittsburgh on the new turnpike, and they had no idea just how steep some of the mountains along Route 30 can be.

By the time I came back out from trying to call Dad and my father-in-law, they were already tinkering with the brakes. They had seen the buses pull in and had started down to the Inn before I called. "They're shot. Wouldn't be safe to move that bus another ten feet," Dad said.

"You're lucky you were headed up the mountain when they went instead of down," Mr. Graffenburg remarked.

My mother suggested that they get the folks off the buses. She and Tinasia prepared lemonade and cookies. I remember being surprised at how many college students came out of those two buses. I remarked to the maestro, "Are there any students left back in Pittsburgh?"

When Mr. Graffenburg and Dad finished looking over the brakes on the bus, they made a call to McConnellsburg and found that they could get brake linings to fit the bus. The maestro was getting a bit nervous. It was obvious that music was his specialty, not bus brakes. "When do you think you can have us back on the road?" he asked my dad and Andrew.

"If we're lucky, tomorrow morning."

"Oh my. . ., well. . ., ah. . ., what shall we do for the night?"

"You can stay right here. It will be tight. There's no way I'm gonna have beds to go around, but if you and your students are not really particular, I'll bet we can feed you and give you a place to rest for the night."

"That's most generous, Sir," Mr. McCambridge continued, "but I'm afraid I have nowhere near enough cash to pay for even a meal. You see, we were to have dinner this evening in Bedford and then offer a concert at the Bedford Springs Hotel."

"I'm not worried about your money. Let's just get your bus fixed, and see what we can do to make you comfortable."

To this very day I don't know how they did it, but Mom and Tinasia set out a meal that was as good as any ever served at the Inn. It was a potluck dinner, where Mom and Tinasia cooked just about everything and anything they could find. My mother-in-law pitched in, and as I recall, everyone got more than their fill and seemed most appreciative.

Dad and Mr. Graffenburg got the brakes off the bus in short or-der, but one of the drums had to be machined, and could not be done until morning. They took the drum to McConnellsburg, and planned to pick it up in the morning.

After dinner, the students congregated outside on the porches. The evening air was warm. The maestro explained that they had been down to Western Maryland College for an exchange concert, and had planned to stop in Bedford to offer a concert in exchange for two meals and one night's lodging. Mr. McCambridge called ahead to the hotel in Bedford. The manager there said they would be welcome to stay the following night. He also called back to the University to let them know where he and his students were. Some of the players had taken their instruments off the bus and were playing a bit. Mem-bers of the choir had gathered around the picnic tables in the back of the Inn and were singing.

Since there were lots of extra dishes, Dad and I got drafted into help-ing. As I looked out the back window of the kitchen, I saw the maestro call all of the players and singers together. I assumed he was explaining what had happened, and that they would be headed for Bedford the fol-lowing day. But then the boys started picking up the benches and tables and carrying them around to the side of the Inn. The maestro stuck his head in the kitchen door and said, "I believe we have thought of a way to repay your tasty kindness. Please join us in about ten minutes on the side of your lovely Inn for a rather informal concert." His nervousness was now replaced with a rather broad smile.

We only had one room rented for the evening, to a businessman and his wife from Columbus, Ohio, so we invited them to join the Graffenburgs and us. That has always been one of the reasons why the Inn is so special. We have learned to make do the best we could, and we have never been afraid or bashful about sharing.

Like I said before, the concert was unlike anything that had ever happened before or since at the Inn. I have heard symphony orchestras play, and I have heard choirs sing but nothing like this. They had arranged the tables and benches on the side porch, like risers. The maestro said they did not have to put on their formal clothes, which was okay with us because we did not feel the need to dress up either. All they had to do was play and sing, and all we had to do was listen.

Once the players and singers were all assembled, and their pitifully small audience was seated, they began. The evening sun was just setting and there was a golden glow to everything. The sun reflected off the instruments of those seated near the front end of the porch. Each selection they performed was more enjoyable than the one before. But the highlight was their final number.

Before playing the final song, Maestro McCambridge introduced the piece. He said it had been written by Ludwig van Beethoven, a German composer, and had been a favorite piece of Thomas Jefferson. He explained, "Music is a beautiful language that transcends the years with unchanging beauty and clarity." And then they began.

Some cars going up and down the mountain had stopped. Folks got out and were sitting in the grass. Mama and Tinasia were going to offer them something to drink, but Dad told them this was a concert for us, and we should just sit and enjoy it. I jokingly said, "There's a stream out back. If they are that thirsty, they can go back there and help themselves!"

For a brief time, the Lincoln Inn, our humble country inn, was treated to the most beautiful concert ever given. The sun seemed to linger just a bit longer than usual on the horizon, just to listen. The members of the University of Pittsburgh orchestra and choir were enjoying their performance as much as we were. Our entire mountainside was absolutely alive.

LUDWIG VAN BEETHOVEN
1770 - 1827

The name of the final piece was *Ode to Joy*. It began slowly, with just stringed instruments playing. I settled back into my chair to enjoy it, when all of a sudden, every instrument seemed to be involved. Without even thinking, I sprang from my chair. I don't think my ears worked any better standing than they did sitting, but in the presence of something that beautiful and that grand, I couldn't sit; it would have been irreverent. In short order, everyone in the tiny audience followed suit.

As the piece continued, the young girls in the choir joined in first. Their voices were absolutely beautiful. Not a bird on that mountain had ever sounded a more beautiful note. Then a young man began to sing, in a voice that carried like the wind.

The movement of the maestro's arms had become so great that they threatened to carry him into flight right off the side porch. Every eye was on him as he brought the instruments and voices together in a most magnificent manner. His silver hair seemed to sense the beat and rhythm of the piece and it moved in time. It was obvious he had conducted this piece many times before and he loved it!

The finale of the piece came, and if I had not been standing there, I would have sworn there were ten thousand voices and ten thousand more instruments playing. I do not know if my senses could have accepted another single note. This was the fullest and most beautiful sound I had ever heard.

When the song ended, we were all left absolutely stunned and entirely speechless. It took some time for the small audience to clap, but clap we did. And then, sensing that clapping was not nearly enough, we all approached the orchestra and choir for a round of hugs and handshakes. I wanted to personally thank each and every one of them, and I believe I did.

During the concert that had lasted about an hour, we had not been paying attention to the crowd that had gathered behind us. I know there were a hundred or more folks who had just stopped and parked along the road. There was a line of cars that went almost out of sight down the mountain toward Chambersburg and another long line that went down the other side of the mountain toward McConnellsburg. A state policeman on a motorcycle had stopped and he was directing traffic. I went out to explain to him that we had not planned to create a traffic problem. Before I could say a word he said, "Wasn't that great!" waving his arms to motion cars along. "You folks enjoy yourselves and I'll keep an eye on things here," he said.

"Great, but make sure you stop in before you leave," I said, as I headed back into the Inn. Again, and I do not know how they did it or where on earth they got the makings, but in short order, Tinasia, Mama, and Mrs. Graffenburg had produced enough lemonade and cookies to satisfy the lot of us.

We had not intended to make any money this evening, but as it ended up there was more than $100.00 left in a small candy dish that Mama kept on the registration desk. I guess someone wanted to leave a buck, others saw it, and followed suit. Dad was uneasy about keeping the money, so he and Andrew used it to cover the cost of the brake linings and having the drum repaired. They gave the rest to the maestro, and told him to treat the students to ice cream once they were back in Pittsburgh.

That night we managed to find enough room and bedding to make the orchestra and choir comfortable. They were a great bunch of kids, and I chatted with some of them late into the night. The state trooper who had kept traffic moving joined us when the crowd broke up. He stayed for awhile, too. Before becoming a state policeman he had attended the University of Pittsburgh for a time. He was born and raised in a small community called Dale Borough out in the western part of the state.

The next morning I drove to McConnellsburg to pick up the break drum, and in no time the bus was ready to go. Though the food supply was all but gone, Mama managed a breakfast before they were on their way.

The maestro could not thank us enough. As he boarded the bus, he said, "You'll hear from me soon, I promise." True to his word, we did hear from him in about three weeks. He sent us tickets for a summer concert to be held on the grounds of the Cathedral of Learning on the campus of the University of Pittsburgh. Dad and I were uncomfortable about closing the Inn even for just a day, but this invitation was an exception. The Graffenburgs offered to stay and keep the Inn open, and Dad told them he would not hear of it. "We've all been invited to Pittsburgh, and we're all going. I won't have it any other way."

The concert in Pittsburgh was great. The maestro had even arranged for us to stay at his home, which was up on Mount Washington, high above Pittsburgh. We all enjoyed the concert, and like the first time we had heard it, we all agreed the final piece was the best. Somehow I wanted to capture it, but in a few moments it was gone, just like it had been when they played at the Inn. I wanted to be able to play it over and over, because I enjoyed it so much. But then again, it may not have been so special if I could have heard it anytime I wanted.

Today, more than forty years later, that informal concert at the Lincoln Inn is still very vivid to me. Believe it or not, there are times that if I stand quietly on the east porch on a warm spring evening, I believe I can hear a faint echo from that night.

CHAPTER

11

The Day the Dam Broke

The day they walked into the Inn, I rubbed my eyes because I thought I was seeing double. It was 1964 and I had turned seventy just the month before. I thought maybe my eyes were starting to play some tricks on me. They looked to be a little older than me, and I later found out that they were both just about to turn eighty. Even after eighty years, they were as perfect a match for each other as I had ever seen.

Of course I had seen twins before, but I had never seen a set of twins that looked any more alike than Mary Elizabeth Wakefield and Elizabeth Mary Stanwix. They were dressed identically, their hair was fixed exactly the same, and they both wore wire-rimmed glasses.

When their husbands came into the Inn, they were as different as day and night. I was glad to see that, because then I knew my eyes were not playing tricks on me after all. While Mr. Wakefield and Mr. Stanwix signed the guest registry, I asked a little about them. Mr. Wakefield said they were from Marietta and the Stanwixs were from Spring Grove, both small towns in Pennsylvania. Both of the Wakefields had been schoolteacher before they retired. Mr. Stanwix was an engineer and Mrs. Stanwix was a schoolteacher. Both of them were retired, too.

I was always interested in what brought folks our way. If they didn't volunteer the information I usually asked. This day, May 29, I didn't have to ask. "We're all headed to Johnstown," Mary Elizabeth said as her husband slid the guest book back across the counter to me.

"The seventy-fifth anniversary of our big flood in Johnstown is on the 31st and we wouldn't want to miss it," Elizabeth Mary added.

"Are you originally from Johnstown?" I asked.

"Yes," they both answered.

"We were born there on May 31, 1884. Our father worked for the Cambria Iron Company. Our house was in Millville down close to the river — that was until the flood," Elizabeth added. I detected a sad note in her voice, so I just nodded in response.

Mary then told me, "We all got out alive, but there wasn't enough left to fill a suitcase. Daddy said as bad as it was, we were lucky, because we all got out alive." I had done some reading about the great flood in Johnstown in 1889. I wanted to ask them some questions right then and there, but it didn't seem like the right time. Tinasia had come out of the kitchen and offered to show them to their rooms. It was just about three o'clock when they checked in, and Tinasia told them that supper would be served at 5:30.

We had many books around the Inn. We were all avid readers. One book that has been around the Inn as long as I can remember is called *Through the Johnstown Flood by a Survivor*. Written by Reverend David Beale, it was published in 1890, just one year after the great Johnstown Flood. I had read the book years before, but that afternoon I got it out again and thumbed through it quickly. To the best of my knowledge, these were the first two Johnstown Flood survivors to stay at the Lincoln Inn, so I wanted to brush up on my history.

Shortly before 5:30 the Wakefields and the Stanwixs came down for supper. There were two other couples and a family of four staying at the Inn as well. That evening Tinasia served baked scrod in lemon pepper butter, new potatoes with flour and bacon gravy, stewed tomatoes with diced green peppers and onions, corn biscuits, and gingerbread with lemon cream topping for dessert.

I was interested to know how much of the flood Mary and Elizabeth remembered, but I was cautious not to ask in case they didn't want to share their memories. However, one of the other guests commented on how much they looked alike and that got the whole dinner conversation started.

"Dad said when they were waiting for me to be born, they had no idea that they were going to have twins," Mary remarked. "Our mother always said she was certain she was going to have a girl, so they settled on the name Mary Elizabeth for me. You see, I was the first to be born. Well, when Lizzie was born just a few minutes later, they hadn't even thought of a second name. So they just switched it around and named her Elizabeth Mary." Everyone chuckled at that.

"They always called her Mary and me Lizzie," Elizabeth added. "And when they referred to us together we were the Shull girls. That was our last name, Shull."

Picking right up on that I asked, "How much do the Shull girls remember about the flood?"

"Plenty, believe me, we remember plenty," Lizzie said.

One of the other guests asked, "What flood?"

"The Johnstown Flood in 1889," Mary said. "We went through it, and lost everything but the clothes on our backs. We're headed there tomorrow for the seventy-fifth anniversary."

"It was such a sad time for everyone," Lizzie said. "It was awful, just awful. We were only five at the time, but we still knew that things were really bad. Our parents kept trying to tell us how lucky we were, but it wasn't until I was an adult that I understood what they meant."

Tinasia had set all the food on the table. Folks were filling their plates and passing food around as Mary and Lizzie continued. They had become the center of conversation. Their husbands, who had certainly heard their stories before, appeared interested nonetheless. I had placed Reverend Beale's book on a small table behind my spot at the dining room table. I wanted to refer to it at some point during the dinner conversation, which I hoped would include their recollections of the flood.

Lizzie was the first to share some thoughts while Mary ate. And as if they had rehearsed it, Mary would then pick up the story while Lizzie ate. They were utterly fascinating. I have heard it said that there is no better source of history than an eyewitness account, and the Shull girls were living proof that this is indeed correct.

"The day started out just fine for us," Mary said. "You see, it was our birthday, and we turned five. The day before had been Decoration Day."

"It had rained most of the day, but we had the parade just like always," Mary continued. "Where we lived in Millville, a little flooding was not at all unusual. Our folks never kept anything good in the cellar of our house, just because the water came up from time to time."

"On the morning of our birthday, May 31, Daddy came home from work early in the morning. He told us that he came home early because it was our birthday. Years later, he told us that the folks who ran the Cambria Iron Company where he worked, sent the workers home to take care of their families," Mary said.

Lizzie said, "I'm sure he didn't want to scare us, but I knew that Daddy and Mother were worried about something. We had an aunt and uncle, our Dad's brother and his wife, who lived over in Brownstown. Their house was up along Gilbert Street along the side of a steep hill. Daddy walked Mother and us over there around 10:00 in the morning."

Lizzie paused, as if recalling the walk, so Mary continued. "The water from the rivers was getting higher by the minute. We walked to the stone railroad bridge over the Conemaugh River where the Little Conemaugh and Stony Creek meet. The water was rushing under the bridge so deep and so fast it sounded like thunder. Lizzie started to cry so Daddy carried her. When we reached the Cambria City side of the river, we walked along the hillside to Brownstown."

"I will never forget how happy I was to get to Uncle Ray and Aunt Blanche's house. It was warm and dry inside. I can still remember the smell of the cake she baked for Mary and me. From the time Daddy called and told them that we were coming, it must have taken us about an hour to get there. Mother had brought us a change of dry clothes. Even now I can remember how good it felt to get dry, warm clothes on and sit by the cast iron stove in Aunt Blanche's kitchen."

"We were only kids, so we had no idea how much danger Johnstown was really in," Mary said. "It was our birthday, we had a cake, and Mother even carried presents along for each of us."

"We each got a rag doll and a fancy hair barrette," Lizzie recalled.

"After we had lunch," Mary continued, "Mother put us down for a nap. Aunt Blanche had an extra bedroom in a loft above their living room and that was where we slept. When we woke up, Mother and Daddy were both sitting on the bed beside us. Mother was holding me and Daddy was holding Lizzie. I could hear Aunt Blanche crying. Uncle Ray tried to tell her that we were safe because we were up on a hill, but she seemed very worried."

"It wasn't until years later that we fully realized what had happened," Lizzie said, pushing herself back from the table.

"Would anyone like some coffee?" Tinasia asked, sensing a break in the story. Several folks said they would.

"Let's adjourn to the more comfortable chairs," I suggested. In short order, we had gathered the larger and softer chairs from the lobby into a circle, so the Shull girls could continue their story. I was fascinated, and since no one went back to their room, I believe everyone else was enjoying the story, too.

Without missing a beat, Mary continued. "You see, at 3:00 in the afternoon, Johnstown was having the worst flood it had ever seen. In some places the water was as deep as eight feet. Then the great South Fork Dam broke. When it did, it sent twenty million tons of water down the valley straight for Johnstown, and there was nothing that could even slow it down, let alone stop it. When that wave of water hit Johnstown, it destroyed everything in its path. There was nothing left standing but a occasional building or house here and there."

Lizzie said, "One of the only buildings left standing in our part of town was the Millville School. Mary and I were to start there in September, but it was nearly Christmas until we got to go to school. You see, they used our school as a place to take the bodies of people who were drowned by the flood waters."

Lizzie paused and so did Mary. Everyone in the room knew that these two elderly ladies were clearly and vividly recalling one of the most horrible events a child could experience. Mr. Stanwix leaned forward, look at his wife, then his sister-in-law, and said, "I've heard you two tell that story a thousand times, maybe more, but each time I do I can't help but feel sorry for the both of you. I suppose I always will." Everyone in the room nodded in agreement.

Mr. Wakefield lightened the mood when he said, "Not me. I never felt bad for either of you, because you got to live in that nifty little house." Both Mary and Elizabeth smiled at his joke. The rest of us had no idea what he was talking about.

"If you're not too tired of our story, we'll tell you about the little house he's talking about," Mary offered. Tinasia, totally enthralled by the story, spoke for everyone in the room when she said, "Oh no, please continue."

"Well, after the flood waters went down and the fires around town died out," Mary said, "thousands of people were without homes. Lucky for us all it was summer. We stayed with Uncle Ray and Aunt Blanche. Daddy and Uncle Ray went back to work as soon as the mills were operating again."

Lizzie added, "I think it only took them a few weeks to get the Cambria Iron working again. You know our mills in Johnstown were among the biggest and the best in the whole world." It was obvious that she was proud of the place where her Dad had worked.

"People all over the world sent money and supplies to Johnstown to help us," Mary said. "The money, as best I can remember, amounted to almost four million dollars. People sent food, building materials, and just plain money. The best things that were sent to us, though, were temporary houses. They called them Oklahoma Houses. They weren't real big, but you could make them comfortable."

Lizzie added that she could remember her Dad walking them down to the railroad tracks the day the first houses came into Johnstown. "They were all folded up. I don't think they were any more than four feet thick, but everything was there – even furniture! There was a cook stove that was also used for heat, a table and chairs, a big bed for the parents, and small cots for the kids in the family. These houses were a story and a half. On the main floor, there was a kitchen and eating area, and a small sitting area, like what we call a living room today. Above the main floor was a loft. It was only about four feet high, so that was where the kids slept."

"I seem to recall Mother telling us years later that they even had bed sheets, blankets, cooking utensils, dinnerware, and silverware," Mary said , leaning back and rocking a bit in her chair. "There was everything we needed to live, which was good, because we had nothing left. And when I say nothing, I do mean nothing. Everything but the clothes on our backs, and the rag dolls and hair barrettes we got for our birthday, was gone."

Mr. Wakefield spoke up. "I didn't live in Johnstown at the time of the flood, but when I met Mary, her family was still living in part of the Oklahoma. They had added on several times in the years after the flood, but that original Oklahoma House was still part of the house on Peelor Street."

"Both of our parents were so thankful for that new start after the flood, they never wanted to part with it," Mary said.

Lizzie quickly added, "If they had sold it or had it torn down they would have felt like they were being rude and ungrateful. So they just added on to it several times when we needed more room. I suppose a lot of people did that, because those little houses were well built."

Knowing that the Wakefields and the Stanwixs were headed to Johnstown the following day, I asked if there was anything special that they did when they went to Johnstown for anniversary observances.

"Oh sure, there are some things we do every time we go back," Lizzie said. We always go to Millville, but it's getting harder to get in there any more since Bethlehem Steel took over Cambria Iron. Everything has grown up so much. We always go up on the inclined plane to Westwood up on Yoder Hill. You get a wonderful view of everything from up there. And then we always go to the cemetery. Its name is Grandview because of the view from where it sits."

Without a pause, Mary said, "That's the saddest part. There are more than seven hundred grave markers in one plot that don't have names on them. You see, 2,209 people died altogether, but in this one plot alone there are more than 770 unidentified. That has to be the saddest part of this whole story."

One of the guests figured that the ladies might be tiring a bit, so he said, "Ladies, thank you very much. Listening to you share your memories, even though they are of a tragic event, was a real treat. You should consider writing a book. There is no history like eyewitness history." One by one, the guests drifted to their rooms. Both Mary and Lizzie stayed behind until everyone else had gone. They answered every question that was asked. I have always been pleased that they chose to stay at the Lincoln Inn, and even more pleased that they chose to share their story.

The next morning the Wakefields and the Stanwixs were among the first to come down for breakfast. The guests once again began asking questions, picking up right where they left off the night before. And just like the night before, both Mary and Lizzie patiently answered every question they could. And just like the previous day, they were both dressed identically. However, for the first time, there was a conspicuous difference. One of them, Mary, was wearing a necklace with a rather large copper coin hanging from it.

I asked her what the necklace was and she reached up and held it. She didn't answer me right away. She just held the copper coin in her hand and appeared to be remembering something, something very pleasant, something she enjoyed recalling. "This belonged to my mother; I mean our mother. Like I said we lost everything in the flood so our mom had no jewelry. Then on one of the days Daddy was working in town, helping to clean up, he found this coin in the mud. You can't read it very well anymore, but it is a large penny from 1802. When he came home that day, he gave it to Mother."

"It must have meant a lot to her," Lizzie said, "because she had a hole put in it and an inscription engraved on the back. She hung it on a gold chain, and for the rest of her life she wore it. I can't ever remember a time when she didn't have it on. Just before she passed away, she gave the necklace to us and told us to share it and take turns wearing it. So that's what we do."

Mary said, "There's no real plan for when each of us wears it, but we give it back and forth several times a year. It means so much to both of us." Mary gently lifted the necklace from around her neck and handed it to me. On the back someone had engraved, "Relic of the Johnstown Flood, May 31, 1889."

"Quite a keepsake," Tinasia said, as she held the coin and looked at it closely.

At this point, it as obvious that Mr. Wakefield and Mr. Stanwix were ready to get on the road. It was going to take them at least two and a half hours to get to Johnstown. There were events scheduled for that day and the next that they did not want to miss. As they were leaving the Inn, I couldn't help but think how lucky these two ladies were that their parents had the good sense to move them out of harm's way 75 years earlier. Unfortunately, many others did not move out of the easily flooded downtown area of Johnstown and as a result perished.

Tinasia and I stood on the front porch of the Inn and waved as they drove west out along Rt. 30 headed for Johnstown. I had nothing particularly pressing to do that day, so I got Reverend Beale's book out again, found a comfortable spot on the side porch of the Inn, and began reading the story of the Johnstown Flood. Since I had had the benefit of listening to Mary and Lizzie tell their story, the whole thing seemed more real to me. It had some additional meaning for me because I now had a connection, a somewhat personal connection, to this tragic event.

I learned a lot from my reading about the Johnstown Flood. A set of numbers about the victims left a lasting impression on me. Even today, I can clearly recall those numbers. As a result of that terrible flood and the fires that followed it, 2,209 people died, 99 entire families were destroyed, and more than 390 children under the age of 10 died. More than sixteen hundred homes were destroyed and almost three hundred businesses suffered losses. For me, these numbers clearly tell the tragic facts of the greatest inland flood ever to hit the United States. Meeting the Shull girls made that tragic story very personal and very real.

Epilogue

In 2001 Tinasia and I had to move off the mountain. I had some health problems and living by ourselves on the mountain did not seem wise anymore. We never did have any neighbors, so when we stopped taking visitors in 1994, we were pretty much by ourselves most days. It was a tough decision, but one we knew we had to make. For a year or so the Lincoln Inn stood empty, and that was the first time it had ever been empty in 107 years. It really bothered both of us, but at 107 and 104 there was not much we could do about it. If the Inn was ever to greet guests again, someone younger than Tinasia and me would be running the place.

When my dad and Tinasia's dad built the Inn, they built it strong and sturdy. Most of the materials were from right there on the side of the Tuscarora Mountain where the Inn stood. Over the years we always took great care of the place. Nothing was ever left to go for too long. Sure there were nicks, scratches, and normal wear and tear over the years, but we always kept after the place. If something broke, we fixed it. If it got scratched, we sanded it down and painted it, and if something just plain wore out we replaced it. We had done some major renovations in 1951 and again in 1973, but the original character and charm of the building were never lost. The day Tinasia and I left the Lincoln Inn it still looked as good to me as it did from my earliest memories more than a hundred years before.

The summer before Tinasia and I left the Inn, a young couple stopped by. I can even remember the date. It was July 8. Their names were Melissa and Brian. They asked if they could look around and that was fine with us. It was nice to have some visitors. Tinasia was making lunch for us, so she put out a little more and we asked them to join us. We had cold meatloaf sandwiches with extra ketchup, sliced tomatoes from my garden and potato soup with fresh bacon. Tinasia had made a wild berry pie the day before, so that was dessert. We enjoyed having them visit. It brought back so many fond memories from when we had guests all the time.

Melissa was a teacher and her husband was some kind of an engineer. He looked at the wiring in the Inn and said whoever had done our work had done a real fine job. He even went down in the cellar to look at some of the original wiring from 1894. He asked me about the cover on the light switch by the front door and we told him the story. He was interested in how the Inn was wired and he seemed fascinated by some of the original light fixtures and lamps. I supposed he was the kind of engineer who worked with electricity, lights and stuff like that. Melissa told us that she was a schoolteacher.

They never told us why they stopped and we never asked them. They just seemed interested in looking at the Lincoln Inn and like always, Tinasia and I were happy to make folks feel welcome. The next summer, we found out why they had stopped. Their visit ended up being what Tinasia and I had been hoping for since we had turned the light off in front of the place the night of my 100th birthday. Let me explain.

You see, even though we were done with the Inn, we knew the Inn could go on. It had a lot more to offer, and someone with some vision and energy could really do something special with the place. Well, on July 28, 2002, we met the folks who had both the energy and the vision. Melissa and her husband Brian called us the day before at Abbott Village, where we moved after we left the Inn. They asked us where we lived, then they asked if they could come to see us. I told them we had a small cottage in a retirement village outside Chambersburg. They asked if they could bring some other folks to meet us. Then they asked if we would mind going up the Inn to show them all around. Well, that was about as nice a thing as Tinasia and I had heard in a long time. Even though we still owned the Inn we didn't get up there much. Gracie's grandson kept an eye on the place and stopped by at least once a week. I sure didn't like that place sitting there empty.

When Melissa and Brian got to our place at Abbott Village, they introduced us to Gregg and his new wife Carrie. They seemed real nice, just like Melissa and Brian. They told us that Gregg and Carrie were teachers over in Lancaster. The six of us went up to the Inn. We had a grand time showing them around. As you know, I like to tell stories about the Inn and the folks who were our guests. These four young folks seemed to really enjoy my stories. When they told us why they wanted to see the Inn, I was glad I was sitting on one of the big chairs in the dining room, for if I had not been, I think I might have fallen over. They wanted to make the Lincoln Inn into a bed and breakfast. Can you imagine that; the place would once again welcome guests.

They told Tinasia and me about their idea, and it sounded better and better the more they talked. I winked at Tinasia. She smiled and shook her head. This was just what we had wanted to hear someone say. They made us an offer on the place that suited us just fine. Tinasia and I had all the money we would ever need, and seeing the Inn open again was worth a million dollars to us.

Well, by the fall of 2002, they were open for business. They didn't exactly change the name, but they did add to it just a bit. It is now called The Lincoln Inn Bed and Breakfast. The colors are the same, they used most of the original furniture, and the only thing they did to the sign out front was add the words "Bed and Breakfast." Once again the Inn was updated without changing the original design my dad and Mr. Grafferburg had come up with in 1893.

They actually bought the place on August 3, 2002, and opened for business on October 8. The afternoon before they opened, they were kind enough to come and pick Tinasia and me up, and take us up to see the place. Oh my, it looked great. Like I said they had given the place a good going over. Even though there were some changes, the original charm had most definitely been respected and preserved.

When we went into the kitchen, it was obvious that someone had been shopping, because there were several bags of groceries on the table. It was just as obvious that no one had made a move to start supper. We were so happy that they had invited us up to see the Inn, but we did not want to hold up their supper. I thanked them for being so kind and started to wish them well when Gregg asked us if we would like to stay for supper. I looked at Tinasia and without saying a word, I knew she would be disappointed if I turned down such a kind offer. Actually, I would have been disappointed if I had turned down this offer. Then Melissa and Carrie gave Tinasia the finest gift anyone could have offered her. Melissa said, "This kitchen had been yours for so many years, we thought you might like to cook one of your favorite meals for us all tonight." Tinasia couldn't even answer. She just hugged her.

Carrie had started to empty the bags onto the large kitchen table. Tinasia looked at what she had laid out and asked her how she knew exactly what to get. Carrie explained that she had found a journal my mother and Tinasia had started to keep in 1927. They had written down a number of the meals we served and some of the comments guests had made. The journals had entries as late as 1978.

One entry in particular had caught Melissa and Carrie's attention when they were going through the journal. It was a meal Mother and Tinasia had prepared on April 18, 1951. That had been my 57th birthday, and for some reason we had a particularly large group of guests that evening. At the bottom of the page, Tinasia had written, "This may be our guests' favorite meal. It is Mac's for sure."

They showed Tinasia the inscription and she said, "It always has been and it still is his favorite meal." With that, Tinasia went to work. With all of the care and attention she had put into so many meals before, she set herself to work. Within no time, the Inn once again had that warm and homey smell that I had enjoyed all my life. The great table in the dining room was set with some of the dinnerware we had bought just after World War I. Shortly after six o'clock we all sat down to eat. Tinasia insisted on serving us, just as she had done so many times before. With some help from Melissa and Carrie, she had prepared what was indeed my favorite meal in my favorite place to eat it.

We started with a lettuce, cucumber, and tomato salad, with a sour cream, vinegar and sugar dressing. The lettuce was finely cut and the cucumbers were peeled and thinly sliced. The tomatoes were still just a little green. They were thinly cut and arranged on the top of the salad. We had ham, green beans and potatoes as the main course along with a side dish of stewed tomatoes and mushrooms. Tinasia had made corn bread and it was still warm, so the butter melted nicely into it. For dessert we had coconut cream pie with extra thick crust.

The new owners didn't seem to be in any hurry, so we relaxed and we talked a lot. Tinasia and I told them bits and pieces of several of the stories in this book and several others. They seemed to really enjoy learning some of the history of what was now their Inn.

When it was time to leave, the girls gave Tinasia the kitchen journal she and my mother had kept for so many years. Gregg and Brian gave me a screwdriver. They asked if I would mind taking the cover off the switch by the front door and turning the light back on again. Needless to say, I did exactly as they asked and I did so with great pride. The Lincoln Inn was once again open for business and the light was once again on to welcome visitors, just had it had been from April 18, 1894, until I turned it off on April 18, 1994.

This had been a wonderful day for Tinasia and me.

The new owners of the Inn, who have become family to Tinasia and me, are in touch with us often. Each year on our birthdays and around Christmas, they have us up to the Inn for dinner. Melissa and Brian now have a son and a daughter, and Gregg and Carrie have a son. I'm happy for this because Tinasia and I had a great life growing up on the Tuscarora Mountain. We're so pleased that Brady Charles, Gabriel Michael, and Olivia Francis will have that same opportunity. We both agreed that the Inn, our Lincoln Inn, is now in the capable and caring hands of folks we love for making us part of their families.

About the Author

Michael R. McGough, was born in Johnstown, Pennsylvania, in 1951. He is a graduate of Greater Johnstown High School, the University of Pittsburgh, Western Maryland College (now McDaniel College), Shippensburg University and Pennsylvania State University.

During his career in public education, he was a teacher, an assistant principal, a principal, and an assistant superintendent. He served in the Bermudian Springs, Carlisle Area and Conewago Valley School Districts. Currently, Dr. McGough is an assistant professor and coordinator of elementary education in the Department of Education at York College of Pennsylvania. He also serves as the director of the College's Professional Development Division.

Since 1976 McGough has been a licensed guide with the National Park Service in Gettysburg. In 2001 he was awarded the rank of Guide Emeritus for his years of service. He is a professional lecturer, a newspaper columnist and the author of several other books. He is married to the former Christine (Tina) Wesner, also originally from Johnstown. The McGoughs have two grown and married children and three grandchildren. The author and his wife currently live in Adams County, Pennsylvania.

THOMAS PUBLICATIONS publishes books about the American Colonial era, the Revolutionary War, the Civil War, and other important topics. For a complete list of titles, please visit our website at:

www.thomaspublications.com

Or write to:

THOMAS PUBLICATIONS
P.O. Box 3031
Gettysburg, Pa. 17325